GUILT Trip

ANNE SCHRAFF

SADDLEBACK
PUBLISHING

Lexile:

HL 710

AR BL: 7.4
AR Pts:

URBAN UNDERGROUND

Bad Blood	No Fear
Dark Secrets	The Stranger
Dark Suspicions	Time of Courage
Deliverance	To Catch a Dream
Guilt Trip	To Die For
Hurting Time	Unbroken
I'll Be There	The Unforgiven
Leap of Faith	Vengeance
The Lost	The Water's Edge
Misjudged	Winners and Losers

SADDLEBACK
PUBLISHING
www.sdlback.com

ISBN-13: 978-1-62250-767-2
ISBN-10: 1-62250-767-3
eBook: 978-1-61247-978-1

Printed in Guangzhou, China
NOR/1213/CA21302313

18 17 16 15 14   1 2 3 4 5

CHAPTER ONE

"Wow," Ernesto Sandoval said to his girl-friend, Naomi Martinez. "I saw a couple cars on Sunday that looked really good. I want to replace the Volvo before graduation. People still think I borrowed the Volvo from my grandpa or something. I want to be driving around the *barrio* in a car with some flash."

"Poor Viola," Naomi said. "She's served you so well. Now to be discarded like a pair of old socks."

"Stop with the Viola stuff, Naomi," Ernesto groaned. "It's just an old car. It's not a pet or anything."

A few months ago when Ernesto was starting to seriously think about replacing the Volvo, Naomi named the car Viola. She laid a guilt trip on Ernesto. Naomi loved Ernesto very much, and she felt good about him driving around in a safe, reliable car.

"I saw this sporty Ford Focus that I liked a lot, and then a silver Corolla caught my eye," Ernesto said. "I've saved enough money for a good down payment so my monthlies won't be too big a burden. With my job at Hortencia's, I'm getting a lot of tips too. I don't expect to get anything for the Volvo. It's too old, and those dents in the back fenders don't look good. They were there when I bought the car, but I was so anxious for wheels I didn't care."

"Oh, so you're not even going to trade her in. She goes directly to the recycler who'll crush her," Naomi said.

"Naomi, *what are you doing* to me?" Ernesto cried, throwing up his hands. "You're making me out to be some kind of a heartless monster for wanting to get a better car. Babe, I'm a young guy. I'm sick of driving around in an old Volvo and having dudes laughing at me. They look over and expect to see some seventy-five-year-old guy with a baseball cap, and instead they see me and start laughing."

"I know," Naomi said, "but she's been faithful." Naomi was a beautiful girl with tawny skin and large expressive violet eyes. Now her eyes were even larger and very sad. Ever since Ernesto first saw the girl in the middle of his junior year at Cesar Chavez High School, those eyes held power over him.

"Okay," Ernesto relented, "I'll give the Volvo to one of those charities that take cars. It'll be better than the recycler, right? Okay, Naomi?"

Ernesto felt like an idiot begging his girlfriend to give permission for him to get rid of his old car.

"Well, at least she'd have a good home," Naomi said.

"Babe, listen. Do me a favor, will you? Stop calling the Volvo 'she.' It's a car. It's made of steel and rubber, aluminum, plastic, whatever. It has no sex. It's not a girl," Ernesto pleaded.

"I suppose after you get rid of her, we'll never see her again," Naomi said, ignoring Ernesto's request.

Ernesto clutched his head, "Naomi, I love you with all my heart, but you're driving me crazy, you know?" he said.

Naomi turned, her magnificent eyes suddenly brightening. "Ernie, I have an idea. We could find her a good home right here in the *barrio*. If you were going to give her to a charity anyway, why not give her to a friend who needs a car and can't afford one? Then we'll still see her from time to time," she said.

"Oh man," Ernesto said, "I can imagine a line forming to get that car. All my homies will be wanting it. They'll be fighting for the Volvo. Paul Morales will ditch his hot Jaguar. Abel Ruiz will dump his cool Jetta. They'll all be vying for old Viola! Oh man. Now you got me doing it too, calling her Viola!"

Naomi laid her soft little hand on Ernesto's bare arm, and, as usual, it sent electric goose bumps through his body. He didn't want to admit it, even to himself, but the girl had him wrapped around her little finger.

"Babe," Naomi said, "leave it to me. I'll find a good home for Viola."

Ernesto looked over at Naomi and smiled. "You do that, Naomi, and meantime, I'm going down to the used car lots this weekend with my homies to scout for cars. I feel like a kid in a candy store. For the first time since I've been going to Chavez, I'll be tooling around in a new set of sporty wheels."

On the next weekend, Ernesto enlisted the help of three friends. Paul Morales, who managed an electronics store, Abel Ruiz who was Ernesto's first friend when he arrived last year at Chavez, and Julio Avila, the best runner on the Chavez Cougar track team.

They all piled into the Volvo on the car hunting expedition.

"*I wonder if she knows*," Julio said softly. He had overheard Naomi humanizing the Volvo and calling it Viola. Now Julio was yanking Ernesto's chain. "I wonder if she knows this might be her last ride."

"What?" Ernesto asked.

"Viola," Julio said. "She must know you're plotting to get rid of her."

"Knock it off, man," Ernesto said grimly.

"Sure she knows," Paul Morales said. "Chicks know when you're getting tired of them and you're getting ready to dump them."

"Dude, the Volvo is not a chick," Ernesto growled.

Abel laughed. "We're just having fun, man. It's kinda cute how Naomi has developed a love for this car. It's like an extension of her love for you, man. It's such a dorky car, but she's right. It's safe and reliable, and she feels good about you driving it. I love my Jetta, but I've been in the garage already a couple times with big bills."

"My old Jag is well-known at the local garage too," Paul admitted.

"Well, I'm going to get a really good used car. Naomi is gonna try to give the Volvo to someone who needs a car in the *barrio*. So it's a win-win situation. I don't think anybody will want the Volvo, so then I'll just donate it to charity."

"Man," Paul Morales said, "I bet if Viola could talk, she'd have some juicy tales to tell about this dude and his chick getting hot and heavy."

"Yeah," Julio said. "Viola has seen it all."

"How would you guys like to get out and walk home?" Ernesto said.

The three boys roared with laughter.

They pulled into a well-stocked used car lot, and Ernesto immediately spotted a Chevy Astro. "Hey, look at the cool van. Roomy too. I wouldn't have to borrow Cruz's hideous van with all the crazy graffiti on it all the time. I've been stopped by the cops twice in that thing."

"Lucky for you Cruz isn't here to hear that, homie," Paul said.

"Look," Abel said, "there's a Chrysler Voyager. It says it can hold seven passengers, and it's only got fifty thousand miles. What a deal."

A handsome man about thirty-five with a thin mustache came walking over. Ernesto just noticed that the car lot was called Vanning with Vann. This guy's name was probably Vann, and all his vehicles were vans. "Hi, boys," he said, "see anything you like? They're all in tip-top shape. We do thorough inspections of every van before we put them out for sale." He held out his hand and said, "I'm Jim Vann."

Ernesto was distracted when a Ford Aerostar van came speeding onto the lot. An angry-looking young man in his twenties was driving it. He jumped from the Aerostar and yelled at Jim Vann, "You ripped me off on this piece of junk, man. I want my money back. I've had this junker for two weeks, and it's been in the garage five times. The transmission is shot, the water pump is leaking."

"Look," Jim Vann said in a reasonably calm voice, "it's a fifteen-year-old van, and you paid less than two thousand. What did you expect?"

The young man came closer. The veins were bulging in his neck. "You crook, why would I want to pay two thousand for a van that doesn't run! I want my money back, and I want it now!"

Ernesto looked at Abel, Paul, and Julio. This was not a good introduction to Vanning with Vann.

Jim Vann turned to the four boys, a smile on his face, "This gentleman is a psycho. I told him when he bought the van that it needed a little work, and he said that was fine, that his friends and he were good at fixing cars," he said.

"You never told me the whole engine was shot! You just said it needed a new battery and a little tweaking," the outraged customer said. "Are you gonna give me my money back or do I get the cops?"

Jim Vann laughed. "Do you see what it says on my sign? I guarantee your money back if you're not satisfied, but you must return the vehicle in ten days. After that, you're on your own. You've had the car for two weeks, so now it's your problem, man. You call all the cops you want, I'm on solid legal ground."

"Four days after I bought the van, I called you, Vann. I left messages. You never answered. You're not getting away with this, you creep." The young man began advancing on the car dealer. "I been fighting a war in Afghanistan to save your freedom, jerk. I got a wife and two babies, and if I haven't got reliable transportation, I'll lose my job! You give me my money back, or I swear I'll take it out on your hide." He grabbed Vann's shirtfront and began shaking him.

Jim Vann turned pale with terror. "Call nine-one-one," he gasped to Ernesto.

CHAPTER ONE

Ernesto moved in behind the disgruntled customer and pulled him away from Vann. Paul Morales helped him. They each took one of his arms, dragging him back.

"Hey, buddy," Paul said, "I hear where you're coming from, but beating up this scumbag is just gonna get you in the slammer, and then your wife and kids got nobody."

"Let me go," the man said, struggling. "He's not gonna get away with doing this to me! I paid him nineteen hundred in cash. It's all I had."

Jim Vann glared at Ernesto. "I told you to call nine-one-one. I want this maniac off my lot," he said. He was scared and upset.

Julio approached Vann. "No nine-one-one, man. We don't need no cops here. We need to talk about this, you know?" he said.

There was a small trailer on the lot where Vann conducted his business. Ernesto, Paul, Julio, Abel, and the young veteran walked into the trailer with Jim Vann.

11

"Listen up," Paul said, "you ever heard of Yelp, Mr. Vann?"

"Of course," Vann said.

"I'm gonna get all my friends to post messages there, dude, saying you're the biggest crook on Washington Street. You're never gonna sell another beater in your life," Paul said.

"You can't do that," Jim Vann gasped. "You can't defame me."

"This young guy here," Julio said, "he's a war veteran. He's a hero. He's been fighting in Afghanistan so jerks like you can live in freedom. We're gonna spread the word, dude. We're gonna picket in front of your rip-off joint that here's a guy who takes a couple thousand from a poor vet who just wants a decent car that runs. Here's a guy, Jim Vann, who sticks it to the soldiers when they come back to the home front."

Jim Vann was pale and trembling now.

"We got a lot of friends in the *barrio,* dude, and when word gets out that you're stiffing a war veteran with a wife and two little kids, you'll have to pack up and run for your life," Ernesto said.

"It clearly says … in the contract … ten days," Jim Vann stammered.

"I think the TV guys will come out and do a story on this," Abel Ruiz said. "I know the councilman for this area, Emilio Ibarra, and he'll be standing right here with the cameras on him, shouting in his booming voice that this guy here steals from veterans just as surely as if he stuck a gun in their faces. The story will be headlined 'Car Dealer Rips Off Veterans Back from Afghanistan.' They'll have promos running for it all evening, right up to the eleven o'clock news."

Paul Morales moved so close to Jim Vann that there wasn't more than a few inches between their faces. "I don't like you, man. When I don't like somebody, I sometimes put serious hurt on them. You hear what I'm saying? You see this rattlesnake tattooed on my hand? If somebody tried to stiff me or somebody I cared

13

about, I'd go out to the desert and find me a rattler. Somehow I'd get that sucker into the crooked dude's bedroom, and likely or not when he put his foot into his bedroom slippers, there's gonna be venom waiting."

Jim Vann turned totally ashen. He grabbed keys from his pocket and stuck one of them into the top desk drawer where he kept a cash box.

It looked like there was about eight or ten thousand in the drawer. Vann counted out nineteen hundred dollars and handed the money to the veteran.

"Thanks, dude," Paul Morales said. "Now you don't need to worry about a rattler greeting you before your morning coffee."

The five walked from the trailer.

"You guys, you were awesome," the veteran said. "I'm Larry Galvan. Thanks from the bottom of my heart. I woulda hauled off and hit the rat, and right now I'd be in the backseat of a police cruiser, cuffed and facing assault charges. You guys … how can I ever thank you?"

"*Por nada*," Ernesto said. "Since you're leaving the lemon here, can we give you a lift home?"

"That'd be great," Larry Galvan said.

"I'm Ernie and these are my friends Julio, Abel, and Paul. I owe you, Larry. I was gonna buy a car here, then you came along and saved me. Hey, I have this old Volvo I was gonna donate. Interested?" Ernesto asked.

"That's good of you, Ernie," Larry Galvan said, "but I need the van for work. Now that I got my money back, I can get me a decent van, one that at least runs!"

After exchanging numbers and dropping Larry off at an apartment on Oriole, Ernesto announced his intention to resume his car search.

"The dude never gives up," Paul said. "You'd think he'd see this as an omen that he should stick with Viola."

"Yeah," Julio said. "Listen to that engine purr. It's like sweet music."

Ernesto ignored his friends. "I'd go back

15

to where I got Viola—I mean the Volvo—last year, but the guy went out of business. I guess he was too honest."

"Yeah," Abel said sourly. "Only the crooks prosper."

"I'm not gonna believe that," Ernesto said.

"The noble and gullible soul has spoken," Paul said. "I'm telling you, Ernie, you can't be getting rid of this car. It's just like you. It's safe, dependable, honest. Viola is your alter ego."

"Look," Ernesto said suddenly, "there's a little used car lot tucked in behind the hot dog stand." Ernesto turned and pulled into the lot. As he got out, he cried, "Look, there's a Nissan Maxima. Shines like a precious stone. It's cool, it's sporty. If it's under five thousand, I can handle the down payment and the monthlies."

A very short Vietnamese man with two little boys trailing him appeared. "You like the Nissan?" he asked, smiling and revealing a gold tooth right in front.

"Yeah, how much?" Ernesto asked.

"Four thousand five," the Vietnamese man said. "Very good car. Perfect condition. Not even a hundred thousand miles yet. Very good deal."

"Hey, that sounds good," Ernesto said. "Can I take it for a test-drive? I'd like to see if it drives as good as it looks."

The Vietnamese man continued to smile. "No problem. You will like this car very much," he said.

Ernesto got in the Nissan after he'd walked around it a few times. Then he said to the dealer, "I like this car a lot. But I'd like my mechanic to take a look at it. Can I give you a couple hundred—like as a down payment—and take it for a couple hours to let my mechanic check it out?"

The man put up his hand, palm facing outward. "No, no, not necessary. You show me your driver's license. That's all. You drive it around. Then take it to your mechanic and see what he says. I think he will like it."

Ernesto asked Abel Ruiz to drive the Volvo home while he got behind the wheel of the Nissan. It was a silver-gray, four-door sedan. It handled smoothly, and it was a blast to drive. Ernesto pulled into the mechanic where his father always took the family car for maintenance. It took him two hours to pronounce the car in excellent condition.

As Ernesto drove home in the Nissan Maxima with Paul and Julio, he said, "There's just one problem. How to tell Naomi. Man, she's gonna make it hard. I know she'll love the Nissan once she gets used to it, but this Viola business is really awful."

When Ernesto had dropped Paul and Julio off, he pulled into his own driveway on Wren Street. The Volvo seemed to look at him with sadness. Ernesto looked away.

Ernesto texted Naomi.

"Babe, got a fab Nissan Maxima. ILU. Ernie."

He got a text back from Naomi.

"LU2. Viola has been adopted! H&K."

Yvette Ozono was a young girl who had been sucked into a brutal gang. She dropped out of Chavez in the tenth grade. When she broke from the gang and got a nice boyfriend, her gangbanger ex-boyfriend killed the boy. Yvette did not want to live. But Luis Sandoval and Ernesto brought her back to Chavez and rescued her. Now she was a math genius. But the family was so poor they could not even afford a beater car.

Naomi Martinez had promised Viola to Yvette and her family.

CHAPTER TWO

Naomi drove Yvette Ozono over to Ernesto's house on Wren Street that evening. Yvette had her driver's license but nothing to drive. Her mother had to carry heavy bags of groceries from the supermarket, and the little ones in the family never got to ride in a car except on rare occasions when friends took them out.

"Ernie," Yvette cried, "you've done so much already for me and my family. I want to pay you something for this wonderful car."

"No, no," Ernesto said. "I was gonna give it away to a charity."

"He was going to dump poor Viola at some mean old recyclers who would have crushed her," Naomi said, giving Ernesto a scornful look.

"Oh," Yvette said, "Viola will have a good home with us. I'll be able to drive Mom when she goes shopping. And I can get around too. I can offer a ride home to a friend instead of always being the recipient of a ride home. Oh, Ernie, we can take little rides in the country. Are you absolutely sure I can't give you some money for this car? It's like a miracle. Naomi said it's so reliable. It just goes and goes. We are so blessed."

Ernesto looked at the girl and smiled. "Yvette, you have no idea what a favor you are doing me to take this car. I'm so happy to pass old Viola onto a family I care about. I'm so proud of you, Yvette, and how much you've accomplished. Whenever I see you driving by in the car, I'll smile."

Yvette threw her arms around Ernesto and gave him a big hug. "You're my hero, Ernie," she said.

"And it'll be nice to see Viola around the neighborhood too," Naomi said. "She likes it in the *barrio*. She'll feel at home at your place, Yvette. Instead of living on Wren Street, she's just moved over to a street nearby."

Ernesto rolled his eyes but said nothing. He couldn't wait to give Naomi her first ride in the Nissan Maxima. He was sure she would forget all about Viola.

On Monday, Ernesto came to Cesar Chavez High for the first time in his Nissan Maxima. Naomi had driven to school in her car. They arrived in the parking lot at about the same time. Naomi got slowly out of her car and came walking over. "Hmmm," she said, "it's smaller than Viola."

"She's a beauty, though, isn't she?" Ernesto said. "Everybody was looking at me as I drove by. They couldn't believe that boring old Ernie Sandoval was driving a hot car."

"It's kinda cute," Naomi said.

"It rides great, Naomi. Harry, Dad's mechanic, checked everything out, and it's

22

in top condition. He said these cars can go for hundreds of thousands of miles. The guy who owned it before kept great maintenance records. Mr. Nguyen gave all the stuff to me. Why, the car even smells like a new car," Ernesto said.

"I think they got some spray now that does that," Naomi said.

Dom Reynosa and Carlos Negrete, who'd been dropouts and taggers before Ernesto and his friends and his father got them back in school, came over.

"Dude, whose car did you borrow?" Dom demanded.

"What happened to the Volvo?" Carlos asked. "Did your grandpa want it back?"

"Yeah," Dom said, "poor old Gramps been taking the bus long enough. Time he had his Volvo back."

"See?" Ernesto muttered to Naomi. "I've been putting up with stuff like this for almost a year."

Dom and Carlos had painted a beautiful mural at Cesar Chavez High, and now they were actually getting paid to put high-class graffiti art on the sides of buildings.

Ernesto turned to Dom and Carlos and said, "I just got this Nissan Maxima, homies. It suits me better, don't you think? I mean it's a cool car, and I'm a young dude and—"

"Nah," Dom said, "that Volvo suited you perfectly, man. That Volvo was you."

"Totally," Carlos agreed.

"Get lost," Ernesto said to his friends, laughing.

"Just wait until you ride in it, Naomi," Ernesto said. "You'll love it. Maybe later on we could go for a ride."

"Yeah, we'll see," Naomi said.

In the middle of the day, right after lunch, the students at Cesar Chavez High noticed a lot of fire engines racing down Washington. They were heading for "auto row" where the used car dealers were clustered.

Everybody got on their cell phones to get the local news.

"Oh, wow," Ernesto said to Naomi, "somebody threw gasoline into the trailer at that Vanning with Vann place where they were ripping off that veteran I told you about. The trailer he used for an office and two cars were wiped out."

"Anybody hurt?" Naomi asked.

"No, they said the lot was closed today because they were repaving. That's a good break," Ernesto said.

"I guess a guy like that who sells beaters that don't even run makes a lot of enemies," Naomi said. "But that's no way to get even. Arson is a terrible crime. You never know when you start a fire where it's gonna go and who's gonna get hurt, like even some poor firefighter."

"I went on Yelp and there sure are a lot of complaints," Ernesto said. "He's a real creep. I couldn't believe that day when the guy realized this poor dude was a veteran, and he wouldn't return his money until we put the pressure on. Paul Morales, especially. He was hinting that he was gonna drop a rattlesnake into Vann's bedroom slippers.

"Larry Galvan, the vet, he sure did me a favor. I might have bought this van I liked and got ripped off too. Right after I bought the Maxima, I called Larry and told him about Mr. Nguyen's place. Larry needs a van, and Mr. Nguyen has several nice ones. Larry picked up a nice van for seventeen hundred dollars," Ernesto said.

"That's nice, Ernie," Naomi said. "You're always doing stuff like that. You don't just look out for your homies. You look out for strangers who need a leg up. That's why I've decided to forgive you for what you did to Viola." Naomi winked at Ernesto then and gave him a kiss.

Ernesto was home from school for about forty-five minutes when he watched the early local news on television. They were showing the spectacular fire that consumed Vann's trailer and the two adjacent cars. Vann himself was interviewed, and when the news reporter asked him if he had any idea who would do such a thing, he said, "It's a mystery to me. I've been selling used vans in the *barrio* for years, and my customers are always satisfied. I consider my customers friends rather than clients. I sell only the best vehicles, and I'm proud of that. I have to believe that this is the work of some madman who had some insane grudge."

"Oh man," Ernesto said, "what a crock. He's nothing but a thief. You shoulda seen how he was treating that poor veteran, trying to keep his money and leave him with a van that didn't work. Larry Galvan was so upset he was ready to fight. Lucky me and my homies came along."

Luis Sandoval looked at his son and smiled faintly. "Paul Morales, Julio Avila, and Abel Ruiz were with you, right? Now I can believe Abel tried to cool things down, but Paul and Julio?" he asked.

"Yeah, me and Paul grabbed Larry when he was hauling off to hit Vann. Then we all went in the office and convinced the crook to give Larry his money back," Ernesto said.

"You guys didn't do anything violent, did you?" Maria Sandoval, Ernesto's mother, asked. "I know Julio and Paul can get …"

"Uh, we didn't beat the guy up or anything, Mom. We just … sorta threatened him that we'd expose his crooked deals on Yelp. Maybe picket the place. He still didn't budge. Then Paul sorta mentioned that when he didn't like somebody, he'd go out in the desert and find a rattler and somehow get it into the guy's house, maybe into his bedroom … you know, by his bedroom slippers. The guy turned white, and he started passing out the hundred dollar bills to Larry then." Ernesto smiled at the memory.

Ernesto's mother sighed. "I try very hard to like Paul Morales, and basically I do, because his heart is in the right place, but sometimes it bothers me that you hang out with him so much."

"Mom," Ernesto said, "the poor vet, he

was so happy to get his money back. You shoulda seen the relief in Larry's face. Mom, this dude did two tours of duty in Afghanistan … there in the worst of the fighting. He's a hero. He's got a wife and two babies, and he's just starting out. He couldn't afford to lose two thousand bucks to a thief. He's finally got a good job, and he needed a van for his work. I'm proud of what Paul did."

Ernesto drove over to Naomi's house after dinner. Felix and Linda Martinez, her parents, came out to inspect the Nissan Maxima.

"Nice car, Ernie," Felix Martinez said. "Real sharp. Time you unloaded that Volvo. This is more like it."

"It's very nice, Ernie," Linda Martinez said. "But it seems funny not to see you driving up in the Volvo."

Naomi appeared then. "It's not the same without Viola, is it, Mom?"

"Come on, Naomi," Ernesto urged her. "Let's go down to Hortencia's for some Mexican hot chocolate."

"Okay," Naomi said, sliding into the passenger seat as Ernesto held the door.

"Look at that, Linda," Mr. Martinez said. "How many young guys would do that? This kid, he's special."

Ernesto smiled warmly at the Martinezes and got behind the wheel. "I love this car," he said. "It handles so beautifully."

"Well, I'm glad for you, Ernie," Naomi said.

They drove onto Washington Street and even as far down as Hortencia's, you could smell the smoky fire from earlier in the day.

When they were seated at the restaurant, Hortencia came over to their booth and said, "I love your new car, Ernie."

"Thanks," Ernesto said. "Boy, that smell of wet burned wood even comes in here, doesn't it?"

"Yeah. It was scary for a few minutes. The fire might have spread to some other businesses. Everybody is saying that dude who ran the van lot was a crook, and he

30

must have made somebody really mad," Hortencia said.

"I was going to buy a van in there myself, when just by coincidence, this young guy comes in. He's been ripped off and wants his money back. He's a veteran of the war in Afghanistan, and this piece of trash, Vann, he's determined not to give the guy his money back. But me and my homies, we sorta encouraged the dude to do the right thing," Ernesto said with an evil grin.

"You bad boy," Hortencia said, laughing. "I won't even ask you what you did, but I hope it was legal."

When Naomi and Ernesto finished their hot chocolates, they drove past auto row. The trailer Vann used was totally gone, but the burned-out hulks of the cars remained. It was an ugly sight.

"Well, whatever happened," Ernesto said, "at least he won't be able to cheat anybody else for a while."

"Yeah, but whoever did that is guilty of a serious felony, Ernie," Naomi said.

"I know," Ernesto said soberly.

"Ernie, you don't think that guy you helped—Larry—you don't think he would have done it, do you? I mean, those poor guys who've been in the war, seen all that violence, the IEDs, suddenly everything blowing up. You don't think he just lost it, do you?" Naomi asked.

"Oh no," Ernesto said. "Larry Galvan is a solid guy. Anyway, he got his money back. He got a good used van from Mr. Nguyen. As far as he's concerned, it's over. The other night, me and Julio and Paul and Abel went to his little apartment on Oriole Street. It's tiny and spartan, but he asked us inside. He's got this great wife and two of the cutest kids. One of them is about three, and the other one just a baby. The wife made coffee and served us Girl Scout cookies they'd bought. They're really nice people. We're friends now."

"That doesn't surprise me, Ernie. Is there anybody you don't bond with in a New York minute?" Naomi said.

Ernesto laughed. "So how do you like the Nissan so far, babe?" he asked.

"It's nice. I like it," Naomi said. "Of course, I don't bond as quickly as you do. I'm still attached to Viola. But give me time. I suppose I'll eventually like this car as much as I liked Viola … *maybe*."

Ernesto dropped Naomi off at her house on Bluebird Street and went in with her for a few minutes to say "Hi" to her parents. Then he headed home, anxious to do some work for his AP History class. All year, he'd been working doubly hard on this class because he really wanted those college credits. Mr. Quino Bustos was an excellent teacher, but very demanding. He was determined that any student getting college credit must do college-level work.

Ernesto had a demanding schedule in his senior year. He was senior class president, he tutored other seniors, and he mentored a freshman. He had his classes and ran on the track team. Along with his classes, he worked more hours than ever at Hortencia's restaurant and tamale shop. And having time for Naomi was a big priority. Nothing was more important than that. So Ernesto was struggling to fit everything in.

When Ernesto came in, his mother was working on the computer. She was outlining her new children's book. Her last book, on lizards, *Don't Blink, It's a Skink,* was doing very well. Her royalty checks were looking good.

When she saw Ernesto, Maria Sandoval turned from the computer, "Ernie, have you got a minute? I need to talk to you."

"Sure, Mom," Ernesto said, sitting down.

"Ernie, you're working so hard, keeping up your grades, earning money at Hortencia's, the senior class stuff, all those projects you've started. It's all wonderful, but now that you have a new car payment on the Maxima, I was thinking. I've got a growing bank account from the books. Why don't I take over your car payment just until the end of the year? Then you could cut back on your hours at Hortencia's."

Ernesto got up from the chair and walked over to his mother, kissing the top of her curly head. "Mom, you're wonderful. I'm so proud of you with all you got to do with Katalina and Juanita and little Alfredo, running the house, shopping, and you still find time to write those great books. Thank you so much for making such a generous offer, Mom, but no," Ernesto said.

"No?" Mom asked. "Why not? Give me one good reason why I can't be using this extra money I'm making to help my son? Ernie, I don't want you to be so busy studying and working that you don't have time to enjoy your senior year. I'd be so happy to help you with the car payment just until the end of the year."

"Mom," Ernesto said, "nobody in the *barrio* has a mom as nice as you. *Mi madre,* you are kind and beautiful. *Mi padre* was very clever in choosing you for his wife. But no, Mom, I don't need any help. I'm doing fine."

"You still haven't given me one good reason why I can't pay for the car, Ernie, just for this year. What would it hurt?" Maria Sandoval asked.

"Because, Mom, if you did that, I'd be less of a man. The other day, I was with Naomi in the Martinez house, and her cousin Carlotta was bragging about her parents planning to buy her a new Audi if she kept up her grades. Naomi said something that really hit home with me. Naomi said that she was proud that she'd paid for her own car, and her parents didn't give it to her. Mom, I'm grateful that you made the offer, honest I am. And if something comes up that I have a problem with the payment for the car, I'll let you know. But right now, I'm fine," Ernesto said.

"Oh, Ernie," Maria Sandoval said, frowning, "you make me sick. It was much easier when you were a little boy, and I'd hide money under your pillow and tell you it was from the tooth fairy, and you'd accept it with no complaint." Mom laughed then and said, "Go do your AP project that you're so worried about. But if you notice somebody messing with your pillow in the middle of the night, don't be alarmed. It'll be me sticking twenty dollar bills in your pillow case."

Ernesto was walking toward his bedroom when his nine-year-old sister, Katalina, screamed. She didn't often scream. Then his seven-year-old sister joined in. Little Alfredo didn't know what was going on, but he started crying.

Ernesto noticed the front yard lit up with eerie red lights, the kind atop a police cruiser.

"The police are here," Katalina cried.

"They're coming to the door," Juanita said.

Maria Sandoval stiffened. Her heart began to beat faster. Ernesto's father, Luis Sandoval, was out late at a teachers' meeting. He was past due home.

CHAPTER THREE

Two police officers were at the door, a male officer and someone Ernesto had seen before, Sergeant Arriola, a female officer.

Ernesto looked at the officers, his heart pounding. "Is this about my dad?" he asked, having the same fear his mother had. Auto accidents happened so quickly, and the consequences could be terrible.

"No," Sergeant Arriola said. She recognized Ernesto and said, "We'd like to talk to you, Ernesto, in connection with an arson case. We understand you may have been a witness at an earlier altercation at the site."

Ernesto breathed a deep sigh of relief and backed up. "Sure, come on in," he said.

Maria Sandoval also looked relieved

that her husband had not been involved in an accident. But she looked apprehensive as well. Katalina and Juanita peered around the corner nervously. It was strange to see police officers in the Sandoval house.

"This is my mom," Ernesto said, turning to Mrs. Sandoval.

"Hello, Mrs. Sandoval," Sergeant Arriola said. Then she got right down to business. "The victim of this arson attack, Jim Vann, told us about a disgruntled customer coming into the auto lot on Saturday morning. He believes this man might be responsible for the crime. We have interviewed Larry Galvan, and he gave us your name and the names of three others who witnessed the incident on Saturday morning. So can you tell me what happened?"

"Okay," Ernesto said. "Me and my three homies, er … *friends*, we went in there to look at cars. I needed to buy a car. While we were looking around, Larry Galvan came in all upset, wanting his money back 'cause the van he got was worthless. Vann wouldn't give him his money back, and we were upset. Larry, he's a veteran of the war in Afghanistan, coming out of two tours of duty with a family to support, and he was ripped off. We, uh … calmed Larry down and told Vann he better give the guy back his money or we'd spread the word that he was a crook, and that he was ripping off heroes who'd just been risking their lives and stuff. Vann gave Larry back his money, and we all left. That's about it, Sergeant Arriola."

Ernesto decided to leave out what Paul Morales had said about finding a rattle-snake in the desert and putting it in Vann's bedroom slippers.

"Were threats made by Mr. Galvan?" Sergeant Arriola asked.

"Uh, well, he was pretty emotional, but I didn't hear threats that I remember. He was just asking for his money back, and as soon as Vann gave him the cash, he was happy. I found an honest car dealer down the street, Mr. Nguyen, and I told Larry about him.

Larry got a great deal down there. He's got a working van now. The thing is, Sergeant, Jim Vann has been cheating customers for a while. Just go on the Internet. He must have plenty of people mad at him. It's just my opinion, but Larry strikes me as a real straight-up guy who'd never commit a crime like arson," Ernesto said.

"Ernesto, why do you think Mr. Vann gave Mr. Galvan his money back when he didn't seem disposed to do that?" Sergeant Arriola asked. Ernesto saw where she was going. She figured the crooked auto dealer was threatened, and she wanted details.

"Well," Ernesto said carefully. "Jim Vann is kinda a little wimp, and me and my friends are all over six feet tall and kinda muscular. We all work out. I mean, when we all crowded into that little trailer and … like asked him in a forceful way that he better not stiff a vet like Larry Galvan … he might have been … you know … intimidated."

Ernesto thought he detected just a trace of a smile on Sergeant Arriola's lips, but she kept it well under control. The male officer then asked a few questions, and they wound up the interview.

"Well, Ernesto," Sergeant Arriola said, "thank you very much for your input."

"Yeah, sure, anytime," Ernesto said. "Glad to help. Good luck in solving the arson. We hate stuff like that around the *barrio*. It's dangerous to everybody."

When Sergeant Arriola and her partner were back in the police cruiser and pulling out of the driveway, Maria Sandoval said, "Whew!"

Katalina finally came out of the hallway, trailed by her little sister, Juanita. They both looked at Ernesto, and Katalina asked, "Are you in trouble, Ernie?"

"No, *mi hermana*," Ernesto said, grabbing his little sister and swinging her around.

"You sure?" Juanita asked.

Ernesto gave his youngest sister a hug and said, "No, I'm fine. Sergeant Arriola just wanted to talk to me because that snake, Jim Vann, is trying to get poor

Larry in trouble over the fire. That figures. Sergeant Arriola wanted the truth, and I gave it to her."

Maria Sandoval looked skeptical. "You left out a few details, Ernie. Like about Paul and the rattlesnake," she said.

"Yeah, of course. I'm not gonna volunteer stuff and get my friends in trouble. Paul was trying to help Larry like we all were. It worked," Ernesto said.

Ernesto's cell phone rang then. "Hey, Ernie," Paul said, "the cops been over there about the arson?"

"Yeah, Paul. Sergeant Arriola and her partner. You too?" Ernesto asked.

"Uh-huh. Seems like Larry gave them our names as witnesses or something. Looks like that scumbag is trying to nail Larry for the fire. The cops talked to Abel and Julio, and they were all cool. Just the basic facts. Nothing about rattlesnakes. So you—" Paul seemed a little worried. He thought maybe Ernesto was such a goody-goody that he spilled everything. Ernesto was insulted.

"Did I talk about the rattlesnake in the bedroom slippers?" Ernesto asked. "Well, duh!"

Paul laughed.

"Sergeant Arriola seemed puzzled about why the little rat caved in and gave the money back when he wasn't threatened, so I said we were four dudes over six feet tall, and when we all crowded into the trailer with Vann, maybe he *did* feel threatened," Ernesto said.

"Yeah," Paul said, laughing again. "Actually I'm glad the creep's place did burn down. Now he can't cheat people anymore. It couldn't have happened to a nicer guy."

"But arson is so bad, man," Ernesto said. "You start flames going, and you never know where they'll end up. Whoever did it has to be a bad dude."

When Ernesto closed the phone, his mother said, "It gives me the creeps to have police officers sitting in my living room. It really scared me when they first came.

Your father is really late coming home, and I thought the worst."

"Me too, Mom," Ernesto admitted. Just then, the living room turned brighter as headlights from Dad's car shone in. In a few minutes, Luis Sandoval came in the front door, clutching his briefcase and looking exhausted.

"I thought that meeting would never end," he groaned, sitting down in his easy chair. "Would you believe Jennie Jones, who teaches health, spent thirty minutes ranting about gum under the desks? The times we live in, the drugs, the crime, the broken homes, and lost kids, and she's still worried about that!" Dad pressed the fingers of his right hand against his closed eyes.

"The cops came looking for Ernie," Katalina announced. "Two of them."

Luis Sandoval jumped out of his chair. "*What?*" he cried.

"No, no, no, Dad," Ernesto said quickly. "They weren't looking for me!" He turned to Katalina who now looked shamefaced.

In her eagerness to report important news,
she had raised false alarms. "Sergeant
Arriola. That lady cop I've met before, she
just wanted to talk to all the guys who were
in Vann's auto lot Saturday. It seems like
Vann is trying to blame the fire on that poor
veteran, Larry Galvan. We told Sergeant
Arriola that Larry didn't threaten Vann. He
just wanted his money back."

Luis Sandoval collapsed back into his
overstuffed chair. "*Gracias a Dios!*" he
cried.

Later on, when Dad had some dinner,
he told Ernesto, "Ernie, you tell that Larry
Galvan to come down to the Veterans Hall
and join up. Most of our members are older
guys from Vietnam and even one from
Korea. I'm one of the younger guys because
I served in Iraq, but I'm graying too. We
need the young bloods to join. There are a
lot of benefits for these kids now, and they
don't even know about them. They think
all we do at Veterans Hall is trade stories
about the Vietnam War or something. Most

of the kids coming out of Afghanistan and Iraq don't even know we exist. Tell Larry to come to the eight o'clock meeting on Thursday night, and we'll give him a lot of information."

"Thanks, Dad, I'll do that," Ernesto said. "He's got two little kids, and they live in a real plain little apartment. I think they'd appreciate some support."

After school, Ernesto and Naomi drove over to the Galvan apartment on Oriole Street.

The apartment was run-down, and the play area for the children was an area of dirt with a few clumps of weeds, one swing, a small slide, and a pile of sand.

Ernesto wondered why Larry hadn't called about the likelihood of the police getting in touch with Ernesto and his friends since he gave the police their names. Ernesto and the others would have appreciated a heads-up on that. It puzzled Ernesto that Larry hadn't called.

Ernesto rang the doorbell and Meg Galvan, her youngest child in her arms, answered. Ernesto and his friends had met her before, but now Ernesto introduced Naomi.

"Mrs. Galvan, this is Naomi Martinez, my girlfriend. She's a senior at Chavez too," he said.

"Hi, Naomi," the young woman said. "Come on in."

"Is Larry home?" Ernesto asked.

"Uh, yeah, he's somewhere around," Meg Galvan said, appearing nervous.

Finally, Larry came down the narrow hallway. "Hey, Ernie," he said. "I'm sorry. I'm so ashamed. You did so much for me, you and your friends, and I gave out your names to the cops and got you involved."

"Hey, don't sweat it, man," Ernesto said. "Everything is cool."

"The cops, they came swarming around here after the fire. Vann told them I threatened to burn down his place unless he gave me my money back. I got so scared.

I thought I'd get busted for arson—then I got desperate and gave the cops your names. I thought you'd back me up. But it was cowardly of me. I didn't even have the guts to call and tell you what I did. I'm so sorry," Larry Galvan said.

"Now you're making me mad, dude," Ernesto said. "You don't call a man who got back from two tours of duty in a war zone 'cowardly,' not around me, you don't."

Ernesto smiled then and grabbed Larry's hand. "Man, there's nothing to be sorry about. I would've done the same thing in your place. Vann is a crook and a liar. Me and my homies all gave the cops the same story. There were no threats. We just crowded in that trailer, and since we're all big guys, the little wimp caved. Now *that's* a coward."

Larry Galvan looked dumbfounded, and then he smiled a little. "Man, that's a load off my mind. I've felt so guilty about involving you guys that I couldn't think of anything else," he said.

"Yeah," Meg Galvan said. "He's been talking about it all the time. Going over and over what he did. You guys were so good to him, and then he told the cops about you. He's been saying that over and over."

"No more thinking about it, dude," Ernesto said.

"I got some fresh-baked oatmeal cookies," Meg Galvan said. "I used a mix, but they're good. You want some with your coffee?"

"Yeah, please," Naomi said. "I love oatmeal cookies."

They sat in the shabby little living room; the toddler sat on his father's lap, and the baby on the mother's lap.

"These cookies are perfect," Naomi said. "Chewy. Just the way I like them."

"Thanks," Meg Galvan said. She didn't look much older than Naomi and already had two children.

"Larry," Ernesto said, "the reason we came over here—my dad was in the Iraq War. He was older than most of the guys, but he was in the National Guard. He was so ticked off by nine-eleven that he volunteered for active duty. He got back okay, thank God, but he's got a scar on his face where an IED almost took out his eye. I told him about you, and he wants you to come down to Veterans Hall on Thursday night and learn about the various programs to help guys like you."

Larry stared at Ernesto. "Me?"

"Yeah, dude, you. Why not?" Ernesto said.

"But I thought they did mostly social stuff for older guys, like bingo or something," Larry Galvan said.

"There's that too, but they're really pushing now to help young vets like you. When a guy is deployed and then comes home, there's a lot of stuff to contend with, getting back into civilian life. There's information on medical and psychological help. When Dad got back from Iraq, he had some serious stress to deal with, and they helped him," Ernesto said.

A strange look came to Meg Galvan's face. "Larry, maybe they could help with … you know, the *nightmares,*" she said, her eyes wide.

Larry Galvan clasped his hands and looked down for a minute, then he said, "It's like I'm back there sometimes. It's not all the time. I can go for weeks, and then I'll hear a siren in the middle of the night, and I'm yelling, 'Anybody get hit?' I some-times scare Meg."

"Look, Larry, just come to the meeting on Thursday night, eight o'clock. They have this informal meeting, and you can learn about what's available. My dad runs the meetings, and you'll like him. Most everybody likes him. He's the go-to guy for everything down there."

Before Naomi and Ernesto left the apartment, Larry Galvan grabbed Ernesto and gave him a bear hug. "Man, you're okay," he said in a husky voice. "You and your buddies did so much for me already, and to think you're still trying to help."

"Dude," Ernesto said, "when we have a football game at Chavez and some of our guys perform well, we call them heroes. The guys who win the World Series—they call them heroes. Everybody wanting their autographs 'cause they're heroes. I'm looking at a real hero right now. Anything we can do for you guys, just holler."

When Ernesto and Naomi got back in the car, Naomi said, "He was almost crying. Did you see that? I saw tears in his eyes. Ernie, you were wonderful. When you do things like this, I'm sorry I gave you such a hard time over Viola. I promise I will try to love this Nissan Maxima, but it will take time."

Ernesto reached around Naomi's shoulders and pulled her against him, kissing her.

At school on Monday, Clay Aguirre came walking up as Ernesto got out of the Nissan. "Hey, so you finally got rid of the Volvo, huh? This is an okay car, I guess. It's better than the Volvo, for sure. But when you drive a car like mine, everything else is chopped liver, you know?"

"Thanks, Clay, I needed that," Ernesto said. "I can always depend on you to brighten my day."

Two police cruisers were in the student parking lot. They seemed to be taking somebody into custody.

Ernesto drew closer to the scene, and he caught his breath in shock. The police were handcuffing Jorge Aguilar, a fellow runner on the Cougar track team and a kid Ernesto had tried hard to keep on the straight and narrow after some missteps. Ernesto's heart sank.

CHAPTER FOUR

Ernesto drew closer to the police cruiser, but not too close. "Hey, Jorge," he shouted. "What's going down?"

One of the police officers turned toward Ernesto and said, "Go about your business. Go to your classes." An officer was loading Jorge into the back of one of the cruisers. The boy looked devastated.

Abel Ruiz was standing nearby, and Ernesto walked over to him. "You know anything about what happened, Abel?"

"Me and Jorge were talking, and all of a sudden the cops showed up, man. Jorge was freakin'. The cops made him sit on the curb, and they searched that old blue beater he drives. They found a laptop in the trunk and some other stuff too. From what I could hear, I think the stuff was stolen from that crooked car dealer's trailer before it got torched," Abel said.

"Oh man," Ernesto groaned. "How did that happen?" A few months ago, Jorge Aguilar was hanging on the corner with some drug dealers, and Ernesto risked his life to get him away from them. If it hadn't been for Paul and Cruz, the drug dealers might have killed Ernesto. They drove Jorge home that day, and Jorge's father gave him a beating. It seemed to straighten Jorge out. He went back on the track team, and he seemed to be doing fine.

"So maybe Vann's place was robbed, and the fire was set to cover that," Ernesto wondered aloud. "But Jorge wouldn't have done that, Abel. Jorge would never pull something like that. It's crazy!"

Abel shrugged. "The guy has a weakness for bad companions. Remember how he hung with Cabron and Simon? He's not a bad guy, but people can talk him into things," Abel said.

Ernesto thought about the nice little stucco house where the Aguilars lived. There was Jorge, his parents, and two sisters. They seemed like a good family. It made Ernesto sick that day when Mr. Aguilar beat the kid, but Jorge seemed to accept it. Nothing like that ever happened in the Sandoval home. It struck Ernesto as unimaginable that his dad would ever beat him. But Naomi's father, Felix Martinez, whacked his boys all the time. Still, Ernesto could not accept that as okay.

Naomi came walking along as the police cruisers pulled away. "What's that all about?" she asked.

"They busted Jorge Aguilar," Ernesto said sadly. "They found stolen stuff in his car, from that used car guy whose place was torched. I can't believe it. We have a track meet tomorrow, and Jorge has been train- ing hard. He was really looking forward to showing his stuff. It blows my mind."

"Somebody must have tipped off the cops that Jorge had the stuff," Abel said. "They came in here like they knew what they were looking for."

"Poor Jorge," Naomi said. "He must be scared out of his wits. He's not a strong guy anyway. His little sister is a freshman here. He always brings her to school. Rachel is her name. I suppose the police called her parents or something, and they'll come get her."

"Yeah," Ernesto said. "Wouldn't it be awful if nobody told her and she'd just be waiting for Jorge this afternoon and not even know?"

"Look," Abel said, "here comes the tow truck. The cops are towing Jorge's car."

"That's so horrible," Naomi said, "that poor family."

Ernesto pulled out his cell phone and called the Aguilar house. A woman answered. From the sound of her voice, she seemed to be crying. "Mrs. Aguilar?" Ernesto said.

"Yes," the woman whimpered.

"This is Ernie Sandoval, Jorge's friend," Ernesto said. "You know what happened?"

"They've arrested my son," the woman cried. "But he's innocent. He didn't do anything."

"Mrs. Aguilar, call Arturo Sandoval. He's my uncle. He's a good lawyer. Call him right away. He'll make sure Jorge gets his rights. He's very fair, and he'll help you. It won't be about the money." Ernesto gave the woman his uncle's phone number.

"*Gracias,*" Mrs. Aguilar said. "*Mi hijo,* he is not a criminal. He's a good boy. There is a mistake. He did not steal anything, and then start a fire. It's a lie."

"I know," Ernesto said. "We'll get Jorge through this. Call my uncle right away."

"*Gracias, gracias,*" the woman said.

At lunchtime, Naomi and Ernesto saw Rachel Aguilar hurrying toward the street. Her hair was flying, and she looked terribly upset.

"Rachel," Naomi called, "do you have a ride?"

GUILT TRIP

"My b-brother," Rachel cried. "They
arrested my brother! Mom called to come
home right away."

"I'll drive you," Ernesto said. "You
don't live far from here. I have plenty of
time to get back to school before the lunch
period ends."

Ernesto didn't know Rachel or her older
sister, Dawn, except to see them around
when he visited Jorge. Dawn was twenty
and recently moved downtown with a
girlfriend.

Rachel climbed in the Nissan, wiping
tears from her eyes with the back of her
hand. "Jorge is a screwup sometimes," she
said. "But he wouldn't do anything really
bad. Jorge would never steal anything.
Somebody must have stuck that stuff in his
car. Oh … this is so awful."

"Rachel, I told your mother to call
my uncle. He's a good lawyer. He'll help
Jorge," Ernesto said.

"We don't have money for lawyers,"
Rachel cried. "Dad only works part time

60

since he was laid off, and we're just scraping by."

"My uncle works *pro bono* where there's a need," Ernesto said.

"What's that mean?" Rachel asked.

"For free. He does that often when people can't afford a lawyer but need one," Ernesto said. "He'll help Jorge."

"I never heard of anything like that," Rachel said. "All people are greedy. Everybody is just out for themselves." The girl had just turned fifteen, but her voice was hard and bitter. Ernesto didn't remember talking to her much when he visited Jorge, but when he did, she didn't seem so hard.

"My sister got a good job downtown," Rachel said. "Right after she graduated from Chavez, she moved out. I hate her for that. She could've hung around a little while and helped us. We got tons of bills we can't pay. She's making good money, but she won't help us. Even if Jorge did steal something, it wouldn't be his fault. He woulda done it for us."

Ernesto didn't know what to say. He couldn't imagine not helping his parents if they needed the money. But he didn't know the whole story. Maybe Dawn had her reasons for moving away.

Ernesto dropped off Rachel at her house and returned to school. He wouldn't have time for lunch, so he wolfed down his peanut butter and raspberry jelly sandwich in the car. Then he ran for his next class.

At the end of the day, Ernesto saw a small group of boys talking in the parking lot. Clay Aguirre had the loudest voice, and he was saying, "Jorge Aguilar sure won't be running in the track meet now."

Ernesto drew closer to the group on his way to his Nissan, and Clay turned and called out, "Jorge Aguilar is one of your homies, isn't he?"

"He's a friend of mine," Ernesto said.

"Well, he's in big trouble," Clay said, seeming to take pleasure in the situation. "I was the one who called the cops, you know. Just doing my duty as a citizen."

Ernesto was shocked. "*You* called the cops?"

"Yep," Clay said in a self-satisfied voice. "Jorge and I were parked side by side, and I didn't appreciate that beater right alongside my Hyundai. I was afraid he'd ding my door, so I went to talk to him. He'd just opened the trunk and then, when he saw me, he quickly tried to close it again. He looked scared. But I grabbed the trunk door to see what he was hiding, and I saw this laptop with the name 'Vanning with Vann' on a little nameplate. And there were a couple cell phones and other stuff." Clay looked smug.

"I asked Jorge what he was doing with that stuff, and he turned pale as a ghost. He said he didn't know it was in his trunk, that somebody put it there. He said he'd just opened the trunk to get another pair of track shoes, and then he saw the stuff. Anyway, I called the cops and told them a kid here at Chavez had stuff probably stolen from the car lot that was torched."

Ernesto looked at Clay with contempt. "You shouldn't have dropped a dime on the guy without hearing more of his side. Jorge isn't a thief, and he's not an arsonist. Somebody could have very well stuck that stuff in his trunk. You jumped the gun, Aguirre. You're so anxious to get people in trouble that you can't wait to call the police," he said bitterly.

"Yeah?" Clay Aguirre sneered. "Well, you're such a wimpy jerk that you'd believe anything just to help your creepy homies."

Ernesto felt a rush of hatred for Clay, but he had to control himself. He was not only a senior, he was senior class president. He had to be better than good. He had to be outstanding.

"It's clear what happened," Clay said to the boys around him, most of whom admired him for his football prowess and for the fact that he drove a fancy car. "Jorge was hurting for money, and he busted into the trailer at the used car lot, stole whatever wasn't nailed down, and then spilled some gasoline around and took off. He's pretty stupid, so he no doubt figured the fire would wipe out everything, and the cops wouldn't even know there'd been a robbery. The guy is in big trouble now. Grand theft and arson. He'll be spending a lot of time in the slammer 'cause he just turned eighteen. No more kiddie court. Now he's tried with the men."

When Ernesto got home, Luis Sandoval had already talked to his brother. "Arturo is trying to get the boy released to his parents at the hearing in a couple days. Jorge told the police he had no idea how that stuff got in the trunk of his car. He said he hardly ever used the trunk because it didn't even lock anymore. He just kept his old track shoes in there. Poor Jorge. He was in a bad way when his parents got down there. He was crying, Arturo said. Arturo is sure he's innocent. My brother has a pretty good instinct about such things. He's not a pushover for young criminals, but he says this boy is innocent."

"It was Clay Aguirre who called the cops," Ernesto said. "He spotted the stuff in Jorge's trunk when Jorge opened it up at school. Clay couldn't wait to call the cops."

"Sounds like Aguirre," Luis Sandoval said.

"Yeah, here was Clay's chance to be a big shot and report Jorge. Like when he called the cops on Cruz and Beto when they were putting in cabinets for Mr. Hussam and got the guys arrested. The only way the nasty little weasel can feel good about himself is if he's screwing over somebody else," Ernesto said bitterly.

At the track meet, Coach Muñoz substituted another runner who wasn't nearly as good as Jorge Aguilar. When the Chavez Cougars ran the relay, Julio Avila was the anchor, Rod Garcia ran the second lap, and the fill-in, Jimmy Valero, ran in Jorge's spot. Ernesto ran the first lap. Ernesto ran a very fast lap, better than he had ever done, and he passed the baton smoothly to Rod Garcia. Garcia ran well, but when he transferred the baton to Jimmy Valero, it almost got dropped. Rod was cursing Valero, blaming him for the fumble that ended up costing the team the victory. Julio Avila ran a lightning-fast last lap but it wasn't enough to make up for the near-fumble. The Cougars were beaten.

Julio Avila kicked the dirt in angry frustration.

"I'm sorry, man," Jimmy Valero said, crushed by his costly error.

Running and winning meant more to Julio than to anyone else on the team. Ernesto could see that he was utterly disappointed, but still he had the grace to force a smile to his face and clap Jimmy on the shoulder. "It's okay, dude. It happens. It happened to me once." Though he was speaking through gritted teeth, Julio Avila showed class. Ernesto was proud of him.

But Rod Garcia, who Ernesto had beaten in the election for senior class president, spoiled the moment. He approached Jimmy Valero and said, "You clumsy idiot. What makes you think you belong on a track team?"

Ernesto moved between the two boys. He didn't say a word to Rod Garcia because he knew if he got started, he might say something he would regret. He looked at Jimmy Valero and said, "You'll get over it. Now you'll train extra hard and do much better. The best runners in the world have fumbled the baton one time or another. And, Jimmy, today you got to see a class act: Julio Avila. Now there's a guy with as much character in his heart as speed in his legs."

Because he had a clean record prior to the discovery of the stolen items in his trunk, Jorge Aguilar was released to his parents at the hearing. A court date was set for the case. Both the police and Arturo Sandoval questioned Jorge as to how those items might have gotten into his trunk without his knowledge.

Jorge said he kept the trunk of his old blue Pontiac beater mostly empty at all times because the lock didn't work. He usually just kept old shoes or some groceries in the trunk. Jorge said he never loaned the car to friends, only to family. The Aguilar family car was an ancient, unreliable Chevy, so sometimes Jorge let his parents drive the Pontiac. Jorge could not recall the last time he looked in his trunk, but he swore that the day at school when he opened the trunk was the first time in his life he had seen the stolen laptop from Vanning with Vann and the other items that did not belong to him.

When asked if he knew of any enemy who would deliberately place stolen items in the trunk of his car, Jorge shook his head. He didn't think he'd ever hurt anybody enough to make them hate him that much.

Even the police investigating the case were tempted to believe Jorge, but as long as there was no explanation for the stolen items being in his car, he was in serious trouble.

Ernesto and Abel Ruiz went over to the Aguilar house on Friday night. Jorge Aguilar had turned eighteen two weeks earlier, but there had been no celebration. The family had no money for gifts or even for food and drinks for a party. Now, with the theft and arson charges hanging over Jorge's head, there seemed even less reason to celebrate, but Ernesto and Abel thought they'd do something to make a special occasion for their friend.

Abel worked out a scheme where it wouldn't look like they were having a special festive meal for Jorge's birthday.

"See," Abel explained very convincingly, "I have been working on a special recipe that I'm going to spring on my boss down at the Sting Ray where I work. So you guys would be helping me out if you tasted the meal and gave me your honest opinion if it's good enough to put on the menu at the restaurant."

Ernesto had loved Abel Ruiz from that first day when he walked over and befriended him as skinny, scared sixteen-year-old from Los Angeles who was a complete stranger at Cesar Chavez High. Of all the students there that day, only one, Abel Ruiz, walked over with a friendly smile and offered to show Ernesto the ropes. But, as Ernesto got to know Abel better, his affection for him deepened. He was a thoroughly nice, compassionate guy. He cared about people deeply. He didn't have Ernesto's looks or Ernesto's brains and charm, but he had about the biggest heart of anybody Ernesto had ever met.

"Well, we would be glad to sample the dinner," Mrs. Aguilar said. "In fact, it would be an honor. And it would be nice to have a fine dinner because not so long ago, Jorge turned eighteen and we did not celebrate."

Mr. Aguilar nodded. "Thank you, Abel, for thinking of us for this experiment," he said.

Abel and Ernesto arrived at the Aguilar house with the fixings for the dinner.

They would be serving seared halibut with winter fruit vinaigrette. The dessert would be one of Abel's specialties, little cream puffs with berry puree. Ernesto had brought some candles for the table and flowers for a centerpiece. It looked very festive. Ernesto had taken the liberty to call Dawn Aguilar and tell her that they were trying to make Jorge feel better by having a birthday dinner that was not a birthday dinner, and could she come?

Shortly before dinnertime, Dawn Aguilar appeared, looking ill at ease. She approached Jorge and embraced him. There was a whispered conversation, and then she sat down.

Rachel glared at her sister and hardly spoke to her at all. Mr. Aguilar spoke to Dawn, his daughter, but only when he absolutely had to. The tension was thick in the room. He had not forgiven his daughter for moving away from home at such an early age.

The bad blood between father and daughter and between the sisters almost squelched what joy there was in the delicious meal. Dawn's mother was grateful that her eldest child had come because she was a mother and she loved her child. Jorge seemed touched that Dawn had come too. There appeared to be a deep bond between Jorge and Dawn, and they embraced again before she left.

Dawn Aguilar hurried out into the darkness then, as if escaping from something bad.

CHAPTER FIVE

Ernesto and Abel had come in Ernesto's Nissan, and they said their good-byes to the Aguilars and then hurried out. Dawn was standing in the darkness, alone.

"Need a ride?" Ernesto asked her.

"No thanks," she said. "My boyfriend is picking me up. I told him to be here at about nine, but we got done early. I couldn't stand being in there for another minute, so I'll just wait here. He'll be along."

Dawn was a tall, beautiful girl, but there was a lot of hurt in her eyes.

"Why didn't your boyfriend come in and eat with us too?" Abel asked. "There was plenty food."

Dawn laughed. "My father despises

Adam," she said. "I think if I tried to bring him in the house, Dad would come after both of us with a meat cleaver. As you probably noticed, there is no love lost between my father and me. The atmosphere in there was so icy you could have hung meat and preserved it. Mom and Jorge are okay with me, but Dad and Rachel think I'm the devil," Dawn said.

"That's too bad," Ernesto said. "I hate to see that in a family."

"Well, it's not my fault," Dawn said. "Dad is very controlling. He didn't want me to date at all in high school, and I went through Chavez sneaking around with boys behind his back. One time he found out. He hit me so hard in the face I thought my cheekbone was broken."

"Not good," Abel said.

"Rachel is his little clone," Dawn said. "She thinks I should still be living at home, kicking in all the money to the family. I do slip money to Mom and Jorge sometimes. I bought Jorge his track shoes. But I deserve a life of my own, and that includes Adam French. He's the love of my life."

"Well," Ernesto said, "we're close friends with Jorge, and we feel terrible about the trouble he's in."

"Dad has beaten him up too. I've seen him whip Jorge, and Jorge just takes it like he deserves that kind of treatment. Sometimes I actually hate my father," Dawn said. "I'm trying to talk Jorge into leaving the house when he graduates too. He's too dumb for college, so he could get a job in a pizza joint or something. At least he'd be away from our father."

"Jorge isn't stupid," Ernesto said. "Now that he's studying harder, he has a B-average. He wants to go to the community college and make something of himself."

Dawn shrugged, shifting her weight from one foot to the other. She tapped her fingers impatiently on her purse. Then, suddenly, she brightened. "There he is. There's Adam."

An old Econoline came around the

corner. It looked like its best days were far behind it. When it came to a stop, the brakes squealed.

"You want to tell your boyfriend to get those brakes looked at," Abel said. "It sounds like they've outlived their usefulness."

Dawn shrugged. "Adam is a struggling actor. He's really short of money. He gets work around town, but they pay like nothing," she said.

Adam French looked out the window on the driver's side. Dawn introduced Ernesto and Abel. Adam was a handsome young man with thick long hair and dreamy eyes. He reminded Ernesto of one of the male leads in that vampire movie. "Hi there, dudes," he said in a laid-back voice. Then he said to Dawn, "How'd it go?"

"Like usual," Dawn said. "Dad and my witchy little sister looked daggers at me all through dinner. Mom was okay, and poor Jorge did his best. All in all, it was a lousy experience. I don't think I'll do it again soon."

Before getting in the car, Dawn turned to the boys and said, "Thanks, guys. Dinner was great. I think you cheered Jorge up too."

Dawn got in the Econoline, and before it moved, both Abel and Ernesto heard Adam say, "I need fifty, babe. Need it bad."

"Tonight?" Dawn said.

"You can get it from the ATM," Adam said. Then they drove away.

Ernesto and Abel stood there looking after the van.

"The guy gives me the creeps, dude," Abel said.

"Looks like he's probably living off her," Ernesto said. "That's why she can't help the family much. I read somewhere that actors can't make much more than a few thousand a year, even if they work steadily on the stage. They get lousy pay if they don't belong to a union, and if they do belong to the union, a lot of theaters won't hire them."

"Maybe that's why Mr. Aguilar doesn't like him for his daughter's boyfriend," Abel said. "How do you spell leech?"

On Monday, Jorge was back in Chavez. One bright spot in his defense was that his fingerprints were not found on the stolen laptop or any of the other items, but he was still the number-one suspect.

At lunchtime, he came down where Ernesto, Abel, Bianca, Naomi, Julio, and Mona Lisa were eating. Carmen came then, hurrying down into the grassy little spot. Jorge looked sad and depressed, but he was struggling to keep up his classwork. Unlike what Dawn thought, Jorge had dreams that went way beyond pizza jobs.

"Dude," Julio said, "if you could only figure out how they got that hot stuff into your car trunk."

"The lock on the trunk works sometimes with the key, but other times it jams, so I don't use it much. I don't know how anybody would've gotten into my car in the school parking lot and put the stuff in," Jorge said.

"Everybody likes you, Jorge," Carmen said. "I never heard one kid say anything bad about you. To try to frame you for some crime like that, somebody would have to hate you."

Jorge ate his ham and cheese sandwich slowly. "I don't know. It's all like a bad dream." He glanced at Ernesto and Abel then. "I bet you guys think I got a real weird family, like everybody hates each other. Dad and Rachel didn't even want to look at Dawn. You guys got nice families, and here are the Aguilars like from a horror movie," he said.

Naomi spoke up, "Jorge, don't feel bad. It's not all sweetness and light in most families. My brothers were bitter enemies with my dad for years. Ernie here had to sneak me and Mom to dinners at little restaurants so we could see my brothers without Dad knowing about it. Then we'd be quaking that Dad would find out. It was like a major international event to get Dad and his warring sons together finally. And miracles happened! We are a family again."

Ernesto laughed. "Yeah, Jorge, we tricked Naomi's dad into coming to Hortencia's for his birthday and out popped the prodigal sons, Orlando and Manny, and we were all wondering if Naomi's dad would haul off and deck them, but like Naomi said, we got a miracle!" he said.

"Now we're all together, Jorge," Naomi said. "Families go through stuff like that, but it's not forever."

"No," Jorge said, "I don't think it'll ever work with my family. Dawn is madly in love with that actor, Adam French. I'm not crazy about the guy either, but Dad hates him with a passion. I think he'd kill French if he could. The guy doesn't make much money acting, and so he sponges off Dawn. He won't get a second job 'cause he's taking acting classes and doesn't have time. He's living off my sister, and that makes Dad furious."

"That's not cool," Julio said. "I think I'm with your father on this one."

"But you know, you guys, Dawn has been a good sister to me. When we were growing up, we were really close. It was like us against the world. There's less than two years between us, and she always took my side. Dad would be mad at me about something, and she'd smooth it over. Even now, she got me some great athletic shoes. She was sort of my protector when we were kids," Jorge said.

"Tough problem," Carmen said. "My dad really didn't like my boyfriend at first, but Paul is a super guy. He's kinda tough and wild, but he's got a good job, and he treats me great. My dad came around 'cause he ended up respecting the really good qualities Paul has."

Jorge continued to look sad. "I don't think Adam French is a really good guy," he said. "I love my family, I love my parents and both my sisters. I mean, I love my dad even though he's mean sometimes. I know that when my dad hit me, he did it to help me become a better person and not screw up. Now look what's happened. I didn't do anything, and I'm in the worst trouble of my life."

"Look, homie," Ernesto said, "you're gonna get through this. I know you, man, and I trust you. You never stole that stuff or torched that trailer. I'd stake my life on it. I know that as sure as I know my own heart. You've just got to do what Julio said. Go back over every day since that fire and place your car. Did you loan it to *anybody* for just a short while? Did you leave the keys laying somewhere, or could another kid have taken the car for a couple hours? There must be something you're forgetting."

A strange look came over Jorge's face. "Sometimes, you guys, I just wish I was dead. That'd be a lot easier than living sometimes," he said.

Abel put his hand on Jorge's back, "Dude, the best is yet to come. You're going places. You're gonna have a good life. This is just a little pothole, dude, and you're gonna make it across," he said.

"Yeah," Ernesto joined in. "Someday you're gonna look back on this bad time and think 'Whoa, who woulda thought my life would be as good as it is now?' "

Jorge smiled, but his friends didn't know if he believed them or not.

After school that day, Ernesto and Naomi went over to see Paul Morales and his brother David. Carmen promised to make her own recipe for bread pudding, and she was going to try it out on Ernesto and Naomi before she sprung it on her family.

Paul Morales had been pretty hard on Jorge Aguilar that day he was hanging with the drug dealers, and Ernesto almost got killed getting him away from them. Ernesto remembered Paul being glad that Jorge was getting a pounding from his father.

Now Ernesto explained to Paul about the stolen laptop being found in Jorge's car and how he might be accused of grand theft and arson. "The kid is innocent, but he's in a bad way," Ernesto said.

"Yeah," Naomi added. "The laptop belonged to that crook Jim Vann, and it looks to the police like maybe Jorge stole the stuff, and then torched the place to cover it up."

"Where's Jorge now?" Paul asked.

"He's back in school. They released him to his parents. My uncle Arturo convinced the judge to do that because Jorge has no record. He looks clean," Ernesto said.

"Jorge Aguilar is an easy mark," Paul said. "He hangs with creeps. Are you sure he doesn't know who did it and just doesn't want to drop a dime on his homies?"

David, who served two years in prison for burglary, nodded. "I hear you. I could've made it much easier on myself if I would have implicated the guys working with me, but I kept quiet and took the whole rap. Maybe Jorge's friends robbed the car lot and stored the hot stuff in Jorge's car just temporarily, and it wasn't supposed to be found there. Now Jorge is being loyal."

"Yeah," Paul said, "it still burns me that my brother rotted in prison for months longer than he had to just to save the neck of some no-good criminal. I'd get the truth out of Jorge. He's not a bad kid, but he's weak. He could have gotten mixed up with another bunch of low-life creeps like when he hung with Cabron and Simon. They did the crime, used Jorge's beater for a storage unit, and … well, how did the cops find it in his car?"

"That's another ugly story," Ernesto said. "Jorge opened the trunk of his car just as Clay Aguirre was strolling by and Aguirre recognized the logo on the laptop. Wouldn't you know the creep called the cops ASAP?"

"Jorge Aguilar is a bad-luck dude, Ernie," Paul Morales said. "You almost got your head kicked in by the last scumbags he threw in with. Maybe you should just let the dude twist slowly in the wind and take his medicine."

Ernesto shook his head. "I can't," he admitted.

Paul shrugged and said, "You want me to corner him and hog-tie him and take him out to the desert and force him to talk? I could do that. I'd just stake him to an anthill and pour molasses on his head."

"Paul!" Carmen screamed from the kitchen.

Ernesto ignored Paul's suggestion. "I can't believe Jorge would put his family and friends through all this to cover up for some creeps he fell in with," Ernesto said.

"Maybe he's afraid to talk," Naomi said. "Maybe he got in with some really bad people, and if he blows the whistle on them, they'll hurt him or his family." Naomi shook her head. "I wish Clay had minded his own business and not called the police on Jorge. The whole thing might have just blown over."

"Maybe I should corner Clay Aguirre and hog-tie *him* and take him out to the desert and stake him to an anthill and pour molasses on *him*. Now *that* would be fun," Paul said.

Carmen emerged from the kitchen. "Sometimes I think I'm in love with a madman," she said coldly.

"I'm sorry, babe," Paul said. "I'll be good."

Carmen brought out the bread pudding and served it. "Now I want the truth. If it isn't really good, then I don't want to serve it for the holidays, so tell me the truth," she said, watching anxiously as they all tasted her dessert.

"The best ever," Paul pronounced. "Am I lucky or what? She's not only smart and beautiful but now she's the best bread pudding maker in the *barrio*. Never mind that she never stops talking. Any chick who can look so good and make me crazy just by kissing my ear and on top of that makes a dessert like this. Dudes, my cup runneth over."

"He's right," Ernesto said. "This is great."

"Ditto," Naomi said.

Carmen turned to Abel. "Now for the acid test. The expert's opinion."

"Magnificent," Abel said.

When they finished eating the sweet custard, Paul Morales said, "Okay, homies, now down to business. Jorge is going down for the count. He's a little jerk, but like you, Ernie, I don't want him put in prison for something he didn't do, and we all know he didn't do it. He's a dim bulb, but he's not a thief and an arsonist. We gotta save him from himself."

Paul paused. Everyone waited to hear his plan. "Now we know he works at that frozen yogurt shop, but we don't know what he does when he's not working or in school. So Cruz and Beto will put him under surveillance. I'll do my part too when I'm not working. We're bound to see him meeting up with some questionable characters if that's what happened. We'll watch his car like a hawk. If we see him going in the Redbird Bar, or some other wild joint, we'll check out who he meets with. If he's hanging with gangbangers or druggies, we'll find the jerk who actually stole the stuff and torched Vann's place. We'll find out who the little jerk is covering for."

"That sounds good, Paul. Thanks a lot," Ernesto said.

"And we'll all keep an eye on Jorge in case some creep tries to contact him at school. We'll keep in touch with each other and report anything promising," Abel said.

"Then we'll all converge on the scene like vultures and strip the skin off the freak who's getting the poor dumb kid in trouble," Paul said.

"What a lovely metaphor," Carmen said, rolling her eyes.

"See," Paul said, "she's not only smart and beautiful and a great dessert maker, but she uses big words like *metaphor*. What a chick!"

CHAPTER SIX

Paul texted Ernesto two days later.

"Nothing yet. JA is keeping to the straight and narrow. No bad companions."

Ernesto and Naomi were at the mall where Naomi was buying a birthday gift for Angel Roma, the freshman girl she mentored. Ernesto started the senior outreach to at-risk freshmen this year. Angel lived with her mother and grandparents. Her grandmother had Parkinson's disease, and Angel had to help out a lot. It was a lot of responsibility for a fourteen-year-old girl.

"You know, Ernie," Naomi said as they stood before the jewelry counter. "Angel's mother is so busy working that she can't spend much time with the girl. Angel's grandfather teaches all day at Chavez, and poor Angel doesn't get much attention." Angel's grandfather was Ernesto's history teacher, Mr. Jesse Davila, and while Ernesto thought he was a good teacher, some other students thought he was too old to be still teaching, and they made fun of him behind his back. Some of that got back to Angel too.

"You think Angel would like this little heart pendant?" Naomi asked. "It looks right for a girl her age."

"What about perfume?" Ernesto asked.

"That's tricky. Everybody has their tastes. If you get something a person doesn't like, it's wasted," Naomi said.

"Yeah, you're right," Ernesto said. "Hey, look at this nice sterling silver chain with a crystal butterfly. That looks cool."

"Oh, I *like* that, Ernie," Naomi cried. "It's much more grown up than the heart pendant, but she *is* gonna be fifteen."

As they were paying for the birthday

gift, Ernesto said, "Did I tell you Paul and his homies were following Jorge? Trying to find out if he's hanging with bad companions again, and Paul texted me. Nothing yet."

"Yeah, Paul said he was gonna do that," Naomi said. "I still can't believe Jorge would take a fall for some creeps and ruin his own future. And what all this is doing to his parents! When we were over there, Jorge's mom looked like she was twenty years older than she is, just from worrying about this."

They headed out to Ernesto's Nissan with the gift-wrapped package for Angel. A few minutes later, as they were back in their own neighborhood, Naomi let out a screech. "Ernie! There's Viola!"

"Huh?" Ernesto gasped, frightened by her loud cry, thinking something had gone wrong.

"Over there, Ernie!" Naomi cried excitedly. "There's Viola! Yvette's at the wheel, and her mom is beside her. Oh, and the little kids are in the back! Oh, that's so sweet. Honk and wave, Ernie!"

Ernesto rolled his eyes before he gently hit the horn and waved out at the Ozono family.

Yvette grinned and waved, and the little ones in the back filled the window, waving too.

"Oh, they look so happy," Naomi said. "Isn't that wonderful? Yvette told me the family hasn't owned a car in five years. They are so happy to be able to get around now."

Ernesto turned down Bluebird Street to drop off Naomi.

Felix Martinez, Naomi's father, was out in the front yard pulling some weeds. Ernesto pulled into the driveway and gave his usual warm greeting to his girlfriend's dad. "Hi, Mr. Martinez. It's good you pull those things out instead of using pesticide to kill them," he said.

"Yeah, Ernie, you know I'm getting to hate the rain. Rain comes and we get weeds.

Weeds all over the place. Look at these big suckers. Their roots reach down to China. Lot of people around here get tired of pulling them, and they just let 'em grow. Makes the street look like a slum. Burns me up. Time comes I can't pull the weeds in my own yard, I'll call the undertaker myself and jump in the satin-lined box," Mr. Martinez said.

"You know," Naomi said, "they've got some spray out now that makes the weeds shrivel up and die, and they say it's not dangerous to the environment."

"Yeah, yeah," Felix Martinez sneered. "They say anything they want. They're a bunch of liars. You spray the poison on the weeds, it gets into the soil, then it gets into the groundwater, goes into the storm drain when it sprinkles and out to the bay where it kills the fish and the birds, everything. You think those crooks who make the poison are gonna admit what it does?"

"But, Dad," Naomi said, "on the label, it says—"

Felix Martinez interrupted her. "Listen to her. This is the girl who made a pet out of your old car, Ernie. She comes runnin' in the house and says she's seen Viola and that the old girl seems to be adjusting to her new family. Bless your heart, Naomi, sometimes I don't think you live in the real world. There ain't no harmless pesticides. I'm gonna be pullin' weeds with these two hands till they plant *me* in the ground."

Ernesto glanced at Naomi. He was a little worried that Naomi had been offended by what her father said, but she was smiling. She had a lot of love for her parents, including her father, and she was willing to take a little ribbing.

"Speaking of pollutants," Felix Martinez said, "some joker went down the street the other day, visiting somebody in the next block, driving this stink bomb of a van. I don't know how it passed smog inspection. I wanted to jump in my pickup and chase the joker down and tell him to get his junker fixed so it don't stink up the whole *barrio,* but he was going too fast. Which is another thing. He was speeding in that piece of trash, and when he went around the corner, his brakes were screaming. The guy is a menace to the road. Pollution, no brakes. It was one of those Econoline vans, good wheels when they're taken care of, but this dude was running the thing into the ground."

Ernesto looked at Naomi. "I bet it was that boyfriend of Dawn Aguilar's. I saw him driving an Econoline with bad brakes." Ernesto said, turning to Mr. Martinez, "The guy is a struggling actor. I guess he can't afford a decent car."

"Ah," Felix Martinez said. "Acting is bunk. He should get a real job. Only a few big shots make enough money acting to live on. The rest are starvin'. I met poor Theo Aguilar the other day at the gas station, corner of Washington, and he was griping about his lousy daughter Dawn. She's a real loser. Turned eighteen, was out of the house like a shot. Has some job downtown serving booze, making big tips. She's no good. Takes up with this creep of an actor. I feel sorry for poor Theo. He tried to put those kids of his on the right track. Kinda reminds me of myself. He's been tough on Jorge like I was with my boys, and they've given me plenty grief. Now poor Theo is worried sick that his boy is gonna go to prison for something he didn't even do. I guess he shoulda whipped the kid harder."

When Mr. Martinez went into the house, Naomi continued talking. Naomi said, "Or maybe he shouldn't have whipped Jorge at all. Maybe he broke his spirit." She was thinking of her brothers, how the family was estranged for years because of Felix Martinez's harsh ways. Fortunately, it came out all right in the end, but Naomi did not approve of how her father treated her brothers.

After dinner that night, Ernesto and his father took a walk. It was a custom of theirs to take a walk together and sort things out.

Father and son walked down Wren Street while there was still some light in the sky. It seemed to Ernesto that it was easier to talk during those walks.

"Ernie," Dad said, "you've always been very loyal to your friends, and that's a good thing. I've always admired that about you. You won't quit on a friend. That's good, but …"

"This is about Jorge Aguilar, isn't it?" Ernesto asked. He knew his father was worried that maybe Jorge was not telling the whole truth about how those stolen goods got into his car trunk. Luis Sandoval did not come right out and say that he didn't feel Jorge was completely innocent, but he was coming to that conclusion.

"Yeah," Dad said. "I like Jorge. I've talked to Theo, his father, and he doesn't think the boy has leveled with the police, with my brother Arturo, with *anybody*."

"Dad, Jorge was one of my first friends when I came to Chavez last year," Ernesto said. "I felt like an alien on a strange planet.

Of course, Abel Ruiz was my first friend, and he really made a difference, but here I was, this skinny kid from LA. I wasn't working out then, and I was pathetic. I was just this wimpy kid, and a couple guys befriended me after Abel. Jorge Aguilar did, and so did Eddie Gonzales. They got me on the track team. I had the feeling that these guys had my back right from the beginning, Abel, Jorge, and Eddie."

"I understand, Ernie," Dad said. "You never forget the friends who were there for you when it really counted. But in spite of that, it shouldn't blind you to the truth of a situation. Theo loves his son, and there were tears in his eyes while he was talking to me. He believes that Jorge knows how that stolen stuff got into his car, and he's not going to talk no matter what it costs him. I just think maybe you've got to face that, Ernie."

Ernesto took a deep breath. "I was so grateful to those guys last year that I thought if they ever needed me, boy, I would be there for them," he said.

"Ernie, do you remember last year when we had those brutal holdups in the *barrio?* After one of them, you saw Cruz Lopez running down the street and suspected he was running from the robbery. You wanted to tell the police, but you held back because Cruz was a close friend of Paul Morales. You put your loyalty to Paul ahead of what you believed you should do."

Ernesto's dad continued, "Then there was another robbery, and the guy was almost killed. Same MO. You were torn with regret. You thought you'd put your loyalty to Paul and his friend ahead of your duty. Yeah, it turned out that Cruz was innocent. But still, you didn't know that when you made your decision. I think that Jorge Aguilar is in such a position right now. He knows he should come clean, but he won't because of loyalty," Luis Sandoval said.

"Dad, Paul Morales and Cruz and Beto are watching the guy. I keep getting texts from them. Jorge goes to work and comes right home. Goes to school. He never stops and talks to anybody. Who is he covering for? I mean, I just don't get it," Ernesto said.

Luis Sandoval shook his head. "Poor Theo is crushed by what's happened to his family. I know Theo has been hard on his kids, and I don't approve of that, but he's a good man. He's a frightened man. He sees these drive-by shootings, like those two kids shot to death coming from the park. He doesn't want his son involved in bad stuff. Theo feels he's lost his oldest daughter. Now he's losing his son. He was almost crying. I didn't know what to say to him. If Jorge does not come clean about what happened, I don't think Arturo can save him. I think he's going to prison for grand theft and arson."

"All I know is that Jorge did not steal those things, and he didn't torch the used car trailer," Ernesto said. "That I know."

Luis Sandoval stopped, turned, and looked at his son. "You know, Ernie, Theo isn't even sure of that. He thinks Jorge could

102

have stolen the laptop and burned down the trailer because he was doing it for somebody else. Ernie, the boy's own father isn't sure of his innocence, but you are. You're telling me you know Jorge better than his own father knows him. That's quite a leap, son."

They turned on Washington and started back toward Wren. Mr. Sandoval threw an arm around Ernie's shoulders. "When I was talking to Theo, he told me his daughter's boyfriend, the actor, he got his Econoline from there. Theo hates the guy Dawn is dating. I don't think he's much of an actor, and he's living off Theo's daughter. Apparently, somebody had driven all the life out of the Econoline, and Vann managed to pawn it off on this actor," Luis Sandoval said.

"The thing has bad brakes. I'm afraid he's gonna kill somebody with that junker," Ernesto said. "Felix Martinez was complaining about it spewing exhaust fumes out too, so it's a total all-around piece of trash."

"I guess Jim Vann doesn't have much of a conscience. He sells all these defective cars and manages to use loopholes to avoid giving people their money back," Mr. Sandoval said. "In a way, it's too bad Clay Aguirre ever saw those stolen goods in Jorge's trunk. I'm not saying people have the right to steal and torch places, but as long as the law doesn't stop a crook like Vann, people are gonna be driven to extreme means."

When they were almost home, Dad said, "Have you got a Plan B, Ernie?"

"What do you mean, Dad?" Ernesto asked.

"What if Jorge doesn't tell what happened, or what if, in spite of your faith in him, it turns out he did the crime? What if he's tried and convicted?" Luis Sandoval asked. "The boy is eighteen, so he could be doing serious time."

"I'd never abandon Jorge," Ernesto said. "I know he's innocent, but if it turns out bad, I'll do what I can for him. But I'm not gonna think that way. I know Uncle Arturo is going to get him out of this."

"*Mi hijo*," Mr. Sandoval said softly, "my brother is a wonderful attorney, but he's not a miracle worker."

It was dark now, and the streetlights were coming on. They paused under one of the streetlights, and Ernesto said, "Dad, Jorge Aguilar is not guilty. I would stake my life on it. He's weak and stupid sometimes, but he would no more steal a laptop and cell phones and start a fire to cover it up than I would."

CHAPTER SEVEN

The following day after school, Ernesto went to Abel Ruiz's house where both boys were studying for an English test. Abel's fourteen-year-old sister, Penelope, came into the room where they were working and flopped down on the sofa. "You guys," she said, "I'm really worried about Rachel Aguilar. I mean, everybody is worried."

Ernesto turned and looked at Penelope. "What's going on with Rachel?" he asked.

"She's freakin', man," Penelope said. "I mean, she's not a special friend of mine or anything, but sometimes she'd come and eat lunch with Angel and me and the gang, but lately she just sneaks off by herself and cries and cries. I think she's having a nervous breakdown or something."

Abel turned too. "Did you ask her if she needed any special help, Penny?"

Penelope shrugged. "What can *I* do? Like if you were gonna get arrested and sent to prison, Abel, what could *I* do? I'd be falling to pieces too like she is. Jorge's court hearing is coming up, and I guess they got the goods on him. It's pretty awful. It's kind of a crummy family anyway. Rachel hates her big sister for moving away and not helping them, and Rachel hasn't anybody to turn to."

"Penny, you need to talk to her," Ernesto said. "If she hasn't anybody to turn to … that's what friends are for."

"I told you she wasn't my friend," Penelope said. "She's always been sorta a loner. But once in a while, she'd hang with us for lunch. I mean, I guess she got ashamed of coming around 'cause everybody thinks her brother is a firebug."

"Do you think Rachel believes her brother is guilty?" Ernesto asked.

"Yeah," Penelope said. "I think so. I mean, everybody knows he did it."

"Penny," Abel said in a harsh voice, "this is the United States of America. You are innocent until proven guilty. Aren't you learning *anything* in history?"

Liza Ruiz, Penelope's and Abel's mother, came into the room. She had overheard the last part of the conversation. "Penelope, I'd rather you didn't have too much to do with that Aguilar girl. If her brother did such a terrible crime, then no doubt she's no good either. I don't want you with her. You know what they say, 'Tell me who you go with, and I'll tell you what you are,' " she said.

"That's right, Mom," Abel said bitterly. "The poor kid is dying of shame and worry, so stick it to her even more by shunning her. If that's not the American way, then I don't know what is. Maybe the freshmen could make a sign for Rachel to hang around her neck that says, 'Stay away from me, I'm evil.' "

"All right, Abel," Mom said in a hurt voice. "You don't have to be sarcastic. Of course, we all feel sorry for the child, but there's nothing we can do. Why compound the tragedy by having Penelope and the other nice girls lose their reputations by … you know? I'm just trying to protect my daughter. If that's a crime, then I plead guilty." Mrs. Ruiz turned then and went back to the kitchen.

When Mrs. Ruiz was out of earshot, Abel, Penelope, and Ernesto talked softly.

"I'll go talk to her tomorrow," Penelope promised. "I'll ask her if there's anything we can do. The kids I eat lunch with are pretty good about stuff like that. Bobby and Richie and Gil, and Angel too. They got good hearts. We'll find Rachel tomorrow and drag her down to the lunch place so she's not alone. I mean, we're not perfect people. None of us are. Who are we to judge anybody?"

Abel walked over and gave his sister a hug.

At school, when it was time for lunch, Penelope didn't see Rachel so she went hunting for her. She found her on a bench behind a eucalyptus tree, just drinking a soda.

"Hey, Rae, come on. We're gonna eat now," Penelope said. "My brother made tortilla wraps for everybody. For you too."

"I think I'll just stay here," Rachel said. "But thanks, Penny." Rachel looked terrible. She had dark circles under her eyes.

Penelope reached Rachel and grabbed her arm. "Come on. Everybody misses you," she said.

"Oh, Penny, I can't face them," Rachel cried. "They all think my brother is a criminal."

"Our gang doesn't," Penelope said. "Come on, Rae. We want you with us."

"Oh, okay," Rachel said reluctantly. "But I feel like they're all looking at me and thinking 'There goes the sister of that guy who robbed the car lot and burned down that building.' "

"Not everybody thinks that," Penelope said. "I don't. My brother Abel and his friend Ernie don't. They know your brother real well, and they think he's innocent."

"Hi, Rae," everybody shouted when she appeared with Penelope.

Rachel started eating the tortilla wrap, and it was delicious, but she still looked sad and embarrassed. Finally, she said, "Lacey Serrano laughed at me this morning and said my brother was going to jail for twenty years because robbery and arson are terrible crimes."

"Lacey Serrano is an ugly witch," Angel Roma piped up. "She and her friend Candy Tellez made fun of my grandma because she has Parkinson's disease. I felt so bad I wanted to die. Don't pay any attention to what she says, Rae. You got to ignore witches. That's the rule."

"Yeah," Richie Loranzo said. "Plenty of kids hassled me 'cause my father is in

111

prison, but my mentor, Ernie Sandoval, said people who do that are so dark and evil in their own heads that they gotta hurt other people so they feel good about their own rotten selves."

Gil Patone, a smart freshman who had taken a liking to Penelope, much to her delight, said, "I've been thinking about what happened with your brother, Rae. I bet he didn't steal that stuff and put it in his car. He wouldn't have brought the car with that stuff in it to school. He didn't know it was in there. I bet he was shocked when he saw it. What happened, I think, is that he loaned his car to somebody, and they did the crime. I bet they stuck the stolen stuff in there, but they didn't think anybody would see it until they could come get it."

"Jorge never loans his car to strangers," Rachel said. "He only loans it to family. Like our family car is a junker. Sometimes it won't go, and Jorge will loan us his car. Or Jorge will loan his car to our sister, Dawn. Dawn doesn't live with us 'cause she's mean and selfish. But her boyfriend has a broken-down Econoline, and sometimes it won't work, so Jorge lets Dawn and him use his car. Dad hates Dawn and her boyfriend, and I do too. So when Jorge loans them his car, he drives over to another street and leaves it where Dawn will find it. Then when she's done with it, she leaves it there and Jorge walks over to get it."

"Maybe the boyfriend is the culprit," Gil said. He loved to read crime novels, and his mind was always working to find the guilty person.

"No," Rachel said. "Dawn's boyfriend is an actor. He's real wimpy. He wouldn't rob a place and torch it."

"Why does your dad hate him?" Penelope asked.

" 'Cause he got Dawn to leave home. And he doesn't make much money so Dawn has to support him. He works at little theaters, and they don't pay hardly anything. He's in something called *It's a Wonderful Life* now, and he'll be lucky to get five hundred dollars for the rehearsals and the nights and matinees that the play is on.

"Dawn works in the bar of a restaurant and makes good tips and stuff, and she gives it all to him. Dad wanted my sister to go to college and be a nurse or a teacher or something, but she met this guy—his name is Adam French—and she went crazy over him. He's really handsome, and Dawn loves him more than she loves any of us. She's forgotten her family," Rachel said.

"I think I saw your sister once," said Bobby Padilla, the student Abel Ruiz mentored.

"You did?" Rachel asked. "When?"

"You know the awards ceremony last week?" Bobby said. "You got an award for English, right, Rae? I saw this pretty girl and a handsome dude watching you get the award. They were standing next to your brother."

"Yeah," Rachel said in a softer voice. "It was nice Dawn came, but I still hate her."

114

"Does that actor guy have a skin disease?" Angel Roma asked.

Rachel turned. "I don't think so. Why do you say that, Angel?"

"His hands looked red and funny," Angel said.

Richie nodded. "I noticed that too. I didn't know that was your sister's boyfriend. I thought he was just some guy, but his hands looked awful, like *burned*."

Penelope didn't say anything. But when Abel came to pick her up after school, she said, "Abel, was Jorge at school today?"

"Yeah, he's right over there," Abel said. "Why?" Jorge planned to jog home today because his Pontiac was having transmission problems.

"We gotta talk to him, Abel," Penelope said.

"What's going down, girl?" Abel asked.

Penelope grabbed her brother's hand and said, "We gotta talk to him now, Abel."

They spotted Jorge getting ready to jog home. Penelope marched up to him and demanded, "Jorge, did you loan your car to your sister and her boyfriend the day the used car lot was robbed and burned?"

Jorge stood there, looking shocked. "*What?* No, what are you talking about?" He turned to Abel. "What's your sister talking about?"

"I don't know," Abel said.

"Rachel told me at lunch today that sometimes you let Dawn and her boyfriend borrow your car," Penelope said. "Maybe she let her boyfriend drive it, and maybe he was the one who did that crime, Jorge."

"That's crazy," Jorge said. "I haven't loaned my car to Dawn in weeks."

Abel noticed that Jorge Aguilar looked pale and shaken. But Abel still couldn't figure out where Penelope was coming from. Where did she get this idea?

"At school last week, at the awards ceremony," Penelope said, "Dawn and her boyfriend came to see Rachel get an English award. A couple of my friends said that this guy—this actor—his hands looked like they'd been burned. I bet he burned his hands starting that fire!"

"Penelope," Jorge gasped, "that's crazy. Adam French is Dawn's boyfriend. He has this skin disease. What's it called? Eczema, yeah. Sometimes it flares up. It looks like his skin is burned, but it's his condition," Jorge started to turn then. "I gotta get home," he stammered.

On their way home, Penelope said to Abel, "Liar was written all over that guy's face, Abel. Eczema, my foot! Don't you get it, Abel? Jorge made that up just now. I bet Jorge loaned his car to Dawn, and the creepy actor took it and robbed the auto lot and torched it. Jorge loves his stupid sister so much he won't blow the whistle on her and the dude she loves. Jorge thinks Ernie's uncle can get him off the hook, and nobody will be the wiser. Then everybody will be home free. But it won't happen like that. Poor Jorge is dumber than our cat!"

"Penny, I just don't know," Abel said, frowning.

"Well, *I* know," Penelope said, grabbing her cell phone. When Ernesto answered, she yelled into the phone, "Ernie, can you meet me and Abel at our house, right away? We're getting in Abel's car to go home."

"I'm headed home too," Ernesto said. "I'll be there."

Minutes after Abel pulled into his driveway, Ernesto's Nissan pulled in behind him. Ernesto jumped out of the car and said, "What's going down?"

"I'm not sure, homie," Abel said. "But Penny has this wild theory."

"Shoot, Penny," Ernesto said, turning to the girl.

Penelope told Ernesto everything she had told Abel. Ernesto said nothing for a few seconds, and then he turned to Abel. "It's worth looking into, man. It may be wild, but it makes a kind of weird sense. Adam French is driving this wreck of an Econoline that he got at Vann's ripoff car lot. So he probably has had it in for the guy for a long time. He's been seething about it, but Vann wouldn't return his money 'cause the crook found a loophole.

"Then Adam hears about everybody complaining about Vann on the Internet, and he gets an idea. Steal some electronics and burn the joint down. But there's trouble. The gasoline fire flares up. He burns his hands. He runs to the Pontiac where he's stashed the electronics and returns the car to Dawn who gives it to Jorge. Adam French figures to get the electronics later, probably after he's gotten his hands treated at Urgent Care, but by the time he can make it over, our friend Clay Aguirre has spotted the stuff. Poor Jorge had no idea it was even in his trunk, but he knows his sister had the car and puts two and two together, and he's not gonna tell on her," Ernesto said.

"So, dude," Abel said, "what you're saying is that Jorge knows what happened, and he'd rather take the fall himself than get his sister in trouble?"

Penelope answered. "See, Jorge thinks he can stonewall and nobody will get punished. He figures Ernie's uncle can get him off the hook because he's innocent. Jorge doesn't think innocent dudes go to jail! And then the crime will just go down as not solved. Don't you get it?"

"It could be," Ernesto said coldly. "That would mean Dawn knows exactly what happened, and she's letting Jorge suffer. She knows Jorge loves her so much and won't turn in her boyfriend for her sake. But she doesn't love Jorge all that much. A lot of chicks would send their family members down the drain rather than lose their men."

"Rachel says she's a creep," Penelope said. "She just thinks about herself."

"But how do you prove a thing like that?" Abel said. "Jorge is gonna go on denying that he loaned the car to his sister. The dude is willing to go to the gallows for his stupid sister and her creep boyfriend."

Ernesto turned to Penelope. "Thanks, Penny, for the information. You did an amazing job figuring this out. I think you're dead-on right."

"My boyfriend, Gil Patone, he sort of put the idea in my head," Penelope said. "He's genius. All of a sudden he goes, 'Maybe the boyfriend is the culprit.'"

Ernesto took a long, deep breath. "I'll do my best to get to the bottom of this. I know one thing—Jorge is my homie, and he's not gonna go to the wall for something he didn't do."

Penelope grinned. "I knew you'd take over," Ernie. "You're the best," she said.

Ernesto got in his Nissan and pondered what to do next. Trying to talk Jorge into breaking his silence was a lost cause. Ernesto knew he needed to go over to Dawn Aguilar's apartment, where the boyfriend probably was, but he didn't want to go alone. He needed someone intimidating to go with him. He needed someone sharp and ruthless who was up for things like this, even eager for them. Ernesto needed someone who was willing to do stuff that would appall most of his other friends.

Ernesto took out his cell phone and punched in the numbers. "Paul?" he said.

"Yeah, Ernie, what's up?" Paul Morales said.

"You've been tracking Jorge for days, you and your friends. Got anything yet?" Ernesto asked.

"Nothing," Paul said. "We've been following the guy, checking all our sources, coming up empty. Jorge has no bad companions, dude. Looks like he's not covering for some gangbangers."

"I may be on to something, Paul. I need backup. It could get dicey, though. Are you on board?" Ernesto asked.

"You got it, man. Jorge is a dim bulb, but he's a decent kid. He doesn't deserve to take a rap for something he didn't do. Whatever you got in mind, homie, I'm on board," Paul said. He sounded eager, excited. Paul Morales was the only friend he had who would be of help in this situation.

"I'll be over to your apartment in ten minutes, Paul. And after I pick you up, I'll fill you in on what's going down," Ernesto said.

Ernesto told his mother he was going over to visit Paul and David. Ernesto felt bad about keeping the true plans he had from his mother, but she would never approve of what Ernesto had in mind. Neither would his father. And Ernesto felt he just had to do this his own way.

Ernesto picked up Paul and filled him in on what Penelope had told him. Paul listened intently, and then he said, "That's a smart kid. I think she just solved the case. I always liked Penelope. She likes me too."

They drove to Dawn Aguilar's apartment near downtown. It was in a cluster of fairly nice condos. The developer had built the condos to sell, but when the real estate market crashed, he rented them. They were stucco with red tile roofs, Spanish style. Dawn made good tips where she worked, and she could afford the fairly high rent.

"Jorge brought me over here once to meet his sister," Ernesto said. "You could tell how much he thought of her. He thought she was really making it, with nice furniture and everything. He was proud of her. I didn't like the chick. I thought she was cold. I didn't even know about the creepy boyfriend then."

"Speaking of the creep, look," Paul said. "There's that rattletrap Econoline parked there. When he went to rob the used car lot, it probably wouldn't start, and that's why he asked Dawn to borrow the poor stiff's beater. Man, what kind of spineless freak lives off his chick like that? Plenty struggling actors get other jobs like bartending or something but he just uses her like you use a dishrag. And she takes it."

Ernesto shook his head. "Dawn told me that she and Jorge were really close growing up. They had each other's backs, she said. I guess the father was always tough, and they covered for each other to avoid his wrath."

"And then she turns around and stabs her brother in the back for the sake of a scum-bag boyfriend," Paul said with disgust. "Me and David were close like that even though we didn't grow up in the same houses most of the time, but there's nobody on earth I'd sacrifice him for. He's my blood. How could the chick do that?"

"Well," Ernesto said, getting out of the Nissan, "here we go. The leech is in there, and it's time for the showdown."

CHAPTER EIGHT

As they walked toward the apartment, Ernesto said, "Now let me do the talking, Paul. If things go sour, then I'll need your *skills*."

Paul laughed in a sinister way.

Dawn Aguilar answered the door. She worked nights at the restaurant bar, and right now she was relaxing in a silk top and lounge pants. She looked very beautiful.

"Oh, hi, Ernie," she said, remembering Ernesto from when he and Abel came to the Aguilar house to sort of celebrate Jorge's birthday.

"Hi, Dawn," Ernesto said. "This is my friend, Paul Morales. Could we come in for a few minutes? This is about Jorge. We're trying to help your brother 'cause, you know, he's in a lot of hot water right now."

Dawn backed up to let them in. "Poor Jorge," she said. "He can't seem to stay out of trouble. I feel so bad that my brother is going through all this. And my ugly father doesn't help. In fact, I blame our father for pushing Jorge into messes like this. He's been so hard on my brother and on me too."

"Who's there?" came a groggy voice from the bedroom.

"Just two of my brother's friends, sweetie," Dawn said. "Go back to sleep, Adam." She smiled and said, "My boyfriend crashes here sometimes. He's working so hard. He's doing this play *It's A Wonderful Life*. You guys ever hear of that?"

"Yeah, the Jimmy Stewart movie," Paul said. "Is your boyfriend playing George Bailey?"

"I wish," Dawn said ruefully. "It's a much smaller part, but important. Adam is such a good and dedicated actor. That's why I let him sleep here. He's struggling so much. Poor guy. He has enormous talent. He's absolutely going to make it big in the theater and then TV. Maybe a television sitcom. That would be amazing."

"Having eczema must be a problem for him," Ernesto said, recalling how Jorge had explained French's red and scaly hands. "Being an actor must make it double hard."

Dawn looked surprised. "What? Where did you get that idea? Adam doesn't have eczema," she said.

Ernesto and Paul exchanged a look. Ernesto said, "Oh, you guys came to Chavez to see Rachel win that English award, and the kids noticed Adam's hands so red and inflamed, and Jorge said it was due to eczema."

Dawn looked worried. "Oh, well, he has a little bit of a problem, but it's getting better."

"Dawn," Ernesto said in a grim voice. "Do you realize your brother is facing a hearing in a few days, and he might be charged with grand theft and arson, both felonies? Since he's eighteen, he'll be tried as an adult, and he could be facing years in prison."

Dawn turned very pale. She sat down quickly, forcing a nervous smile to her lips. "Oh, he'll never be put on trial. He has this wonderful attorney, your uncle, Ernie. Mr. Arturo Sandoval. He's a legend in the *barrio*. I've heard so many wonderful things about him, how he's helped other guys in trouble. I'm sure he'll take care of everything, and Jorge will be fine," she said.

"My uncle has been able to help kids accused of minor crimes, but this is serious business. The laptop and cell phones were worth thousands of dollars. Cash was taken too. It wasn't found in the car, but Vann claimed he lost four thousand dollars that was there," Ernesto said. "If this goes to trial, there's a good chance he'll be convicted and sent to prison."

"Yeah," Paul chimed in. "My brother spent two years in the slammer. That's gonna be really hard on a kid like Jorge. Scrawny little scared dude like him, always been under his father's thumb, got no fight in him. The other cons will have him for dinner. You got a clue what happens to a young guy like that? My brother went through hell. This is probably gonna be the ruin of Jorge's life."

Dawn looked increasingly distraught. She wore some gold bracelets on her wrist, and she was nervously spinning them around. "I'm sure … it won't … be … like that," she stammered in a robot-like voice.

There were noises from the bedroom. An unshaven and annoyed Adam French came down the hall barefoot, in his pajamas. "How can I get any sleep with all this yakking going on?" he demanded. "What are these dudes doing here? I gotta go to work in a couple hours!"

"How's your eczema, man?" Paul asked. "The medicine helping any?"

French glared at Paul. "I got no eczema. What are you talking about?" He glanced down at his hands. They were red. "Who are you? What're you doing here?"

Paul had been sitting on the edge of the sofa but now he got up quickly, panther-like. He sprinted over to Adam French and grabbed his arm, pushing back one sleeve, "Oh, this guy is right. No eczema. He's been in a fire. Those are burn scars. What happened, man? You playing with gasoline and it flared up on you? That can happen. Bad business fooling around with gasoline and matches. It's not easy to start a fire." Paul released the man's arm, shoving him back a few feet.

Adam French looked shocked. "It was a grease fire ... on the stove. We were making french fries," he gasped.

"Yeah, I remember," Dawn cried, her eyes wild. "I put too much oil in the kettle. It was so stupid ... and ... and Adam tried to put out the fire. He was so brave ... but ... but ... he got burned."

"Listen up," Ernesto said in an infuriated voice. "First the phony eczema, now the phony french fries. Jorge is my friend, and he is not going down for what you guys did. He's had my back in some tough scrapes, and now I've got his. The kid is not going to prison for what you did, French. I swear it."

"You get out of my apartment," Adam French screamed. "Both of you, get out of my apartment, or I'll call the cops and have you thrown out!"

"It's not your apartment for one thing, dude," Paul Morales said. "It's her apartment—that idiot girl over there who works nights serving drinks so she can support somebody who claims to be a man, but isn't, who's living off some stupid chick who hasn't the decency to stand up for her own brother, for her own blood. You're a leech, French, you're a lousy leech, and you're an arsonist and a thief too, and you are going down, man."

"Get out," Dawn cried. "Get out this minute!"

"You kinda disgust me, lady," Paul

Morales said. "A chick who'd turn her back on her own little brother for some creep like this."

"I'm calling the cops," Adam French said, "and having you charged with trespassing!"

"Dude, you go for it. You're nailed. When we tip off the cops, they'll check your fingerprints against that stolen laptop and the cell phones. The only acting you're gonna be doing is in a cell block, acting like you're not scared when you will be scared."

"No punk is gonna come in here and try to pin a crime on me," Adam French yelled. He approached Paul Morales and made a big mistake. He took a swing at him. Paul dodged the blow and grabbed the other man, throwing him down to the floor, face-down. Paul straddled the actor's back and touched the back of his neck with the tip of a ballpoint pen.

"This is a switchblade, man," Paul said. "You feel that, dude? I'm taking you out right now if you don't admit what really happened. Your girlfriend gave you Jorge's car, right? And you took it down to Vann's lot and busted in and robbed the dude and then to cover it up, you torched it. Admit it!"

Dawn rushed to the couch to get her cell phone. Ernesto was faster. He grabbed the cell phone and hurled it into the fireplace where it broke apart. Dawn clutched her cheeks and began sobbing.

"I'm gonna cut you, man," Paul threatened. "It's gonna be a pleasure."

"Vann's a crook," Adam French gasped. "He sold me that Econoline, no brakes, shot transmission. Wouldn't give me my money back. I just took what was mine. I did the whole neighborhood a favor. What's the big deal? He's got insurance. I already paid for the crime with these burns. I've been miserable!"

"The big deal, you cockroach, is that you're letting an innocent kid take the rap," Paul said, getting up and letting French rise too.

Ernesto called the police. It took them a long time to understand the whole story, but eventually they took Adam French into custody on suspicion of grand theft and arson.

After searching French's room in the apartment, they found some small items taken from Vann's lot, items he hadn't put in Jorge's car. The electronics taken from the trunk of the car were in the evidence room at the police lab, and French's fingerprints were found on them. A check of the nearest Urgent Care facility revealed that French had come in suffering burns on his hands from a gasoline fire just twenty-five minutes after the fire. He told them it happened while he was trying to repair his car.

When the police left with Adam French, Dawn Aguilar sat on the couch with her face in her hands.

"You want me to call somebody?" Ernesto asked. "Your mother or—"

"You've done enough," she said without looking up.

"Dawn, you knew all along that your boyfriend did this, didn't you? You knew your kid brother was getting put through the wringer, and you kept your mouth shut," Ernesto said. "I can't get my head around that."

Finally, the girl looked up, "Haven't you ever loved someone so much that you would do *anything* in the world for them?" she cried. "I love Adam with all my heart. He's my *life*. Don't you understand what I'm feeling?"

"Shame?" Paul ventured. "That'd be good."

"Who is this brute?" Dawn asked, glaring at Paul. "He's surely not a student at Chavez. Where did you get this bully?"

"He rented me at the brute factory," Paul Morales said. "I'm sort of like your stinking boyfriend. I can be hired. Except sometimes I do stuff for free when my heart is really in it, like this tonight. Lady, if I were you, I'd go to my brother and beg his forgiveness. You know what? He knew all the time what went down. He knew he loaned you the car, and that you and your rotten boyfriend had it at the time of the robbery and fire. Jorge knew what happened, and to spare you and the creep, he went through all this. He loves you that much, you ungrateful chick. How are you gonna live with yourself?"

Ernesto and Paul left then, walking to the Nissan.

"Thanks, man," Ernesto said. "I couldn't have done it without you and that's no bull."

"Of course not," Paul said, getting into the passenger side.

"I'm stopping at the Aguilar house on the way home, okay, Paul?" Ernesto said.

"Good," Paul said.

Ernesto called Uncle Arturo with news of what happened, and he was delighted. He called the Aguilars immediately. He said there were still some legal hoops Jorge had to jump through, but he'd be all right now.

When Ernesto and Paul came through the door of the Aguilar house, Rachel threw her arms around Ernesto and cried, "Thank you!" Then she hugged Paul, who she didn't even know. Arturo Sandoval had told the family these two boys had saved Jorge.

Jorge appeared, followed by his parents. Mrs. Aguilar was crying for joy. "*Gracias a Dios*," she kept saying, over and over. Theo Aguilar had been crying too, and he put his hand out to Ernesto and Paul, thanking them profusely.

Jorge stood there, looking bewildered. Finally he said, "Dawn ... my sister ... is she ... okay?"

Paul Morales looked at Ernesto and shook his head.

The three boys—Ernesto, Paul, and Jorge—stepped outside the Aguilar house.

"Dude," Paul snarled, "the chick knew all along what happened, and she didn't care about you!"

"Love, it makes people crazy sometimes," Jorge said. "He was the first guy she fell in love with. She didn't have boyfriends

138

in high school. We were … always close, me and Dawn. She must be torn up now. She's all alone. If only … if only I could bring her home. I mean, she needs support now."

Paul Morales grabbed Jorge by the shoulders, "I want to shake you, man. I want to shake some sense into you. Your sister was fine with you taking the fall for that scumbag. *Don't you get it?*"

Ernesto moved alongside Jorge and said softly, "Go on inside, homie, and give your parents and Rachel a lot of hugs. Rachel helped us a lot with this. Be with your parents, man. They've been through a lot. They love you, Jorge. They died a little inside every day you were under suspicion. Your father said if something happened to his only son, then he didn't want to live anymore. Homie, go in there and be with the people who love you."

Tears ran down Jorge's face, and he went inside and closed the door after himself.

As Ernesto drove toward Paul's apartment to drop him off, he said, "Maybe Dawn will come around. Maybe she'll realize what she did and come around."

"She's bad to the bone, dude," Paul declared.

"You're sure of that, huh, Paul?" Ernesto asked, glancing at his friend.

"Oh, sure. No chick with an ounce of good in her would have screwed her own brother like that. Brothers are blood. Boyfriends come and go. What Jorge needs is a nice chick to get him over this. You ought to look around, Ernie, and find him somebody like Carmen. Not that there's anybody around like her, but *sorta* like her. You know what I mean. When I first met Carmen, I was like a thug, man. Being with Carmen has softened me. Made me much nicer, don't you think?"

Ernesto couldn't help laughing. "You mean there was a time when you were worse than you are now, homie?" he asked.

"Oh, yeah," Paul said. "Like the Paul

Morales of a few months back would have probably killed that actor. Might have strangled him then and there. Wouldn't have *pretended* that sharp thing at his neck was a switchblade; it *would have been* a switchblade. I'd have cut him, a little bit at least. Listen up, dude, that's progress. I owe a lot for that to Carmen, and to you too, Ernie. You're so kind and compassionate that you'd never beat anyone to a pulp, Ernie. I aspire to be more like that. It makes me sick most of the time, but I do admire it too."

Ernesto laughed again, and he and Paul fist-bumped before Paul went inside his apartment. Ernesto called Naomi and told her what happened, and then he headed home.

When Ernesto pulled into the driveway on Wren Street and went inside, he found that his mother and sisters had already gone to bed. They had absolutely no idea what Ernesto had been up to. They thought he was just visiting over at Paul's, probably eating Carmen's bread pudding.

Luis Sandoval was up, though, watching the eleven o'clock news. Ernesto was glad his father was still up.

Dad looked at Ernesto and said, "I talked to Arturo, just briefly. He told me Jorge has been cleared, thanks to you and Paul."

"Yeah," Ernesto said, sitting down on the couch opposite his father. "Jorge doesn't have anything to worry about now. He was completely innocent. Turns out, he loaned his car to his sister Dawn, and the creepy guy she's in love with took the Pontiac, went down and burglarized the auto lot trailer, and then burned it down. He got his hands burned in the process, and so he returned the car to Jorge with the hot stuff still in the trunk, planning to get it later."

Ernesto paused then and pulled out his cell phone. He dialed Abel. "Dude, we got Jorge off. Put Penelope on," Ernesto said.

"Should I wake her up?" Abel asked.

"Yeah," Ernesto said.

In a few seconds, Penelope was on the cell phone. "Ernie—what happened?"

"You did it, girl," Ernesto said. "You and your BF, Gil Patone. You were right. Because of what you told me, we nailed the creep and got Jorge off the hook."

Penelope's scream was so loud, they hardly needed a cell phone. You could probably have heard it all the way from Sparrow to Wren Street.

Ernesto laughed and returned to his conversation with his father.

"How did you guys do it, Ernie?" Dad asked.

"Oh, it's a long story, Dad. It has to do with eczema and french fries, and a bunch of little freshmen playing detective," Ernesto said.

"Come again?" Dad asked, smiling.

"Me and Paul went over to Dawn Aguilar's apartment, and we encouraged this creepy actor boyfriend of hers to come clean. We had the goods on him," Ernesto said.

"Paul didn't do anything illegal, did he?" Luis Sandoval asked.

"Illegal? Paul?" Ernesto asked in mock shock. "I couldn't have done it without him, Dad. He's one of a kind. Dawn was really angry at him. She called him a brute and wanted to know where I got him. Paul told her I rented him at the brute factory."

Luis Sandoval laughed, then he said, "*Mi hijo,* I really had doubts about Jorge. I wasn't sure he wasn't implicated in that crime. But you were sure he was innocent. You were right and I was wrong. You knew your friend's heart. He's lucky to have a friend like you."

"Thanks, Dad, but you know what blows my mind? Paul's too. Jorge is worried about what will become of Dawn. After what she did, covering up what her boyfriend did and letting Jorge go through all that. Still, all he said was 'Is Dawn all right?'"

"Love," Luis Sandoval said. "There is no logic to it."

CHAPTER NINE

On a Sunday night, when Ernesto was with Naomi in the hills overlooking the city, his cell phone rang. They had just been admiring the incredible tapestry of lights from the city and the suburbs, which seemed to flow seamlessly into the starry blackness of the night.

Ernesto resented the intrusion. He appreciated the convenience of cell phones, but sometimes he wished they had never been invented. Like now. "Yeah?" he said.

"Ernie, this is Dawn Aguilar," the voice said. "Did I call at a bad time?"

Ernesto felt like saying anytime she called would be a bad time. He could not forgive her for what she had done to Jorge, even though Jorge forgave her at once.

"What's up, Dawn?" Ernesto asked.

Naomi's eyebrows went up. She realized that Ernesto didn't want to be talking to anybody on the phone right now. It was a magical night, and they were listening to their favorite music and snuggling.

"I haven't talked to my parents, or Jorge, or Rachel," Dawn said. "I feel so terrible. I don't want to wake up in the morning. Is there any chance that you would talk to me, Ernie? Jorge always said you were willing to help anybody but maybe …"

Ernesto was torn. He shared Paul Morales's opinion of Dawn Aguilar. But there was a part of him that found it hard to resist helping someone in dire need, even if they didn't deserve the help. "Dawn, let me get back to you in ten minutes," he said. When he disconnected the call, he looked at Naomi and said, "She says she needs someone to talk to. Maybe she's feeling regret or something. Babe, I'm no counselor. I don't know what I'd say to her. I almost hate her."

Naomi reached over and covered Ernesto's hand with her hands. "Babe, if she wants to talk to you, then you should do it. I know it bothers you. But she's a human being. She might be going down for the count, Ernie. You don't want to hear that she was found floating in the ocean or something."

"Naomi, would you come with me?" Ernesto asked. "I'm not sure I could do it alone."

"Sure," Naomi said. "I know the family. I know Jorge. How many times has he eaten lunch with us at school?"

Ernesto dialed Dawn back. "Dawn, when do you want to talk?" he asked.

"Could you come to my apartment now? I'm all alone," she said.

"My girlfriend Naomi is with me," Ernesto said. "She knows Jorge and Rachel too. Is it okay if we both come?"

"Yes," Dawn said. "I just need some

advice. I'm drowning, Ernie, and I don't know what to do."

They drove down from the hills and headed for Dawn's apartment. "Naomi, how do you figure this girl? Jorge claims he and Dawn were inseparable as kids. She even bought him his athletic shoes a few months ago. How do you figure it?"

"It's hard, Ernie. I love you more than anybody I've ever known, but I love my brothers too. I can't imagine the pain if I had to choose. It would tear me into pieces, but the thing here is, she didn't do what was right. She knew her brother was innocent and her boyfriend did it. No matter how much you love someone, you can't hurt someone else for the other's sake. That's how I was brought up. Maybe Dawn was brought up a different way," Naomi said.

"Yeah. What are we supposed to say to her?" Ernesto said.

"Listen to what she has to say and go from that," Naomi said.

When a red light stopped them, Ernesto

leaned over and kissed Naomi. "Thanks so much for not bailing on me, babe," he said.

"Ernie, if you had to go meet some one-eyed aliens, I'd go with you," Naomi said.

They parked outside Dawn's apartment, and when they rang the bell, Dawn answered immediately.

"Dawn, this is my girlfriend, Naomi," Ernesto said.

"Hi, Naomi," Dawn said in a drained voice. "Can I get you guys anything?"

"No," they both said almost at once. They wanted to get this over with as quickly as possible.

Dawn sat down opposite the sofa Ernesto and Naomi sat in. She clasped her hands, looked down for a minute, and then looked up and said, "I know you think I'm an evil person, and maybe I am. I know it was stupid and blind of me, but I didn't think Jorge would be charged. I didn't guilt trip him into staying quiet. I thought he'd get off. I'd like to think that if he had actually been charged, I would have come forward and told the truth. I'd like to think that, but maybe not. I heard once that love is a drug, and I guess I was high on Adam. I knew what he did, but only after he did it. I didn't think it was so bad to cheat a cheat. I was in a dream world. I thought that if I just didn't saying anything, everything would turn out all right."

"Jorge would have been charged," Ernesto said.

"I know that now. I talked to his lawyer. He said they would have thrown the book at Jorge. Grand theft is serious, but arson is even worse," Dawn said.

"Yeah," Naomi agreed. "When you deliberately start a fire, you could end up murdering somebody."

"The thing is," Dawn said, beginning to cry, "I want to go home. I know my father hates me, but Jorge texted me that he still loves me. I'm sure my mom would take me back. I could make peace with Rachel eventually."

"Call them and say you want to talk, Dawn," Ernesto said. "Call your mom."

"Do you think Jorge meant what he said?" Dawn asked. "He texted me that he cares about me, but he must be bitter. I mean, how could he not be bitter?"

"He's forgiven you, Dawn," Ernesto said. "Don't ask me how that's possible, but that's how Jorge is. You guys must have had an incredible bond as children, and he can't get that out of his mind. You know what he said to me? He said, 'If only I could bring Dawn home.'"

Dawn cried for a few minutes, then she said, "I'm not a monster. I just never thought Adam would do such a thing. Jorge loaned me the car, and Adam asked me if he could use it 'cause the Econoline was busted again. When Adam came home with his hands all burned, I didn't know yet what had happened.

"Then I heard about the fire on the news. I noticed Adam all of a sudden had a lot of cash, and when I asked him where it came from, he just laughed. Little by little, I got more suspicious. Adam told me to take

151

Jorge's Pontiac to the regular spot where we always left it, and I took the bus home. Jorge came and got it and drove to school. I guess he never looked in the trunk. Adam never came right out and told me what he did, but I knew in my heart. I can't deny that. I kept lying to myself that somehow everything would be okay. Haven't you ever done that, Ernie?"

"No," Ernesto said. "I've got the kind of mind that would not let me lie to myself."

Naomi hadn't said much since they'd arrived here, but now she said, "I know what you mean, Dawn. I lied to myself for a year and a half about this boyfriend I had. I was really in love with him. He was rude and mean to me sometimes, but I always made excuses for him. He'd make me do some of his assignments for him, and I felt guilty because that was cheating, but I did it anyway. I felt so bad about myself, but I kept on doing it. He'd yell at me in front of our friends, but I'd tell myself he was under so much stress that he really didn't mean it. Because I loved him so much."

Dawn looked gratefully at Naomi.

"And then this guy, Ernie, came along, and I found out what real love is. Real love makes you feel good about yourself, not bad. Real love never hurts. Ernie helped me see the light, and I dumped the jerk. But not before he hit me so hard in the face that I had a bruise for two weeks. Even then, I sort of made excuses for him. I thought, 'I must have made him so mad … it was my fault.' Clay was like a fever I had, a disease, and when I dumped him, the fever broke and I was healthy again."

"Was this Clay guy your first love, Naomi?" Dawn asked.

"Yeah," Naomi said.

"Adam was mine," Dawn said. "Dad never let me date in high school. And then Adam came along, and I fell for him like a ton of bricks."

"Dawn," Naomi said, "call your mom. Talk to Jorge. They'll work together to arrange a way for you to come home. It'll be hard at first. Jorge will be on your side because that's Jorge. Your mom will be too, because that's how moms are. Rachel will come around and maybe even your father eventually. My dad was bitterly angry at my brothers for a long time, but Ernie and I worked out a reconciliation."

"But your brothers didn't do anything as horrible as I did," Dawn said. "I could have helped Jorge but I left him twist in the wind just to spare my boyfriend blame for what he did."

"Dawn," Naomi said, "my oldest brother decked my dad. He had his reasons, but we won't go into that. But to my dad, that was the unforgivable sin. You do not deck your father. But we got past that. Now my brothers come to the house, and they laugh and kid with Dad."

"Hey, here's a plan," Ernesto said. "How about if Abel Ruiz arranges to make a nice dinner at your house to celebrate Jorge getting off the hook. Naomi's family got reconciled over a nice dinner. There's something about good food that smooths over bad feelings. Abel could cook up something amazing, and your parents and Rachel will be there, and Jorge could invite you as his special guest. I think it might work. I'll be there with Naomi too, and we'll help all we can."

"Oh," Dawn said, "it would be so wonderful if it worked. I don't deserve this. I know it. But it would be so great if I wasn't rejected by my family for the rest of my life!"

"Well, Dawn," Ernesto said, "I'll be honest with you. You probably don't deserve it, but Jorge does. He isn't going to be happy if you're never part of the family again."

Naomi then said, "Dawn, have you been in touch with Adam French since he was arrested?"

"Yes, I tried to talk to him, but he didn't want to talk to me. We said a few words. He's really bitter. He said it's all my fault that this happened. He said I've ruined his life. He told me if my brother's crazy friends hadn't come over and practically forced him to confess to the crime, then he wouldn't be in jail now," Dawn said. "I guess I still love him, but we're finished. Adam is facing a lot of prison time and …"

"Well," Ernesto said, "I'll be in touch, Dawn. I'll talk to Jorge and Abel and see if they like my idea, and then we'll go from there."

There was hope in the girl's eyes. "I appreciate this more than I can say," she said.

As Ernesto and Naomi walked from the apartment, both of them had misgivings.

"You think it'll work, babe?" Ernesto asked as he slid behind the wheel.

"Oh, Ernie," Naomi said. "I know Jorge, but I don't know Mr. Aguilar. My own dad was bitter about the boys during that long estrangement, but I always knew he loved my brothers. Even in the darkest times, when he was calling them bums and whatever, I could see it in his eyes that he loved them, and if need be, he would die for them. I don't know if Mr. Aguilar's heart is like that."

When Ernesto presented the scheme to Jorge at school, he was excited. "I won't tell Dad that Dawn is coming. He might veto it before it even happens. I'll just pretend my parents and me and you and Naomi and Abel will be there. I'll act like it's Rachel and me, but not Dawn. Then, right before we start to eat, I'll go to the door and say 'Tah-dah' and in will come Dawn. Maybe Dad will be mad, but … oh, Ernie, this is a wonderful idea. I'll have my sister back. I've felt so awful with all this going on. I know you and Paul Morales, and maybe Abel too don't like her, but you didn't know her before she was that creep's puppet. She just became a different person, Ernie. But now that he's gone, she's Dawn again."

"Well, Jorge, we'll do our best," Ernesto promised.

Jorge grabbed Ernesto and hugged him. "Dude, you're the best. You never gave up on me. As long as I'm breathing, homie, you're number one in my book."

Late Friday afternoon, Ernesto, Naomi, and Abel arrived at the Aguilar house with all the fixings for the big meal. It was announced as a special celebration for Jorge now that his terrible ordeal was over. Dawn had been tipped off to wait on a side street, and when Jorge called her on his cell phone, she should make her appearance.

When Ernesto, Naomi, and Abel arrived, Theo Aguilar gave them a warm smile. "This is so kind of you," he said. "We are so grateful for our son being cleared, and it is all because of his wonderful friends. Jorge is so lucky, so blessed to have such good friends. It was the darkest moment of my life when Jorge was arrested, and now the sun shines in my heart. *Mi hijo* is safe!"

"Jorge is our *amigo,* Mr. Aguilar," Ernesto said. "Me and Abel and Naomi, we all eat lunch every day with Jorge at school. He is part of our family!"

"Yeah," Abel said. "We all felt terrible when Jorge was in trouble. It's a big load off everybody's mind."

Abel then headed for the kitchen with Naomi to start dinner. Abel would do the cooking, and Naomi would be his faithful assistant.

Ernesto looked around at the other members of the Aguilar family. Mrs. Aguilar had deep, dark circles under her eyes. The long ordeal had taken a toll on her. She had not slept well in a long time. And then there was the sad reality that although her one child was home safe from his ordeal, her other child, Dawn, was still outside the family circle. Mrs. Aguilar was a mother, and she could not forget her eldest child no matter what she had done. Mrs. Aguilar had despaired over whether she'd ever have her daughter in the family again, and that grieved her and made it impossible for her to fully enjoy the celebration.

Rachel was just wildly happy to have her big brother out of danger, and being fourteen and embittered against her sister, she didn't miss her at all.

Abel made one of his favorites, carne asada. He made many exotic dishes featuring seafood and chicken, but everybody seemed to love carne asada. Soon the delicious aroma filled the small house, and the family gathered at the table with their friends.

"*Mi esposa,*" Mr. Aguilar said gravely, "Please, say the blessing."

The family and the four teenagers bowed their heads for the blessing. Mrs. Aguilar expressed thanks for the good food, for those who cooked it and shared it with them, and for God's blessings on them all. She prayed for her husband, for Jorge and Rachel and Ernesto, Abel and Naomi, and then, almost inaudibly, she prayed for Dawn. Her husband did not look pleased.

Jorge excused himself from the table and went into the hall to make the call. He returned to the table and, within minutes, there was a knock at the door.

Jorge jumped up and went to the door.

"Dawn," he cried in pretended surprise. "Come in. We have said the blessing, but we haven't started to eat." Jorge gave his sister a hug. She was so nervous she was shaking. She was almost afraid to look at her father. Her eyes downcast, she let Jorge lead her to the table.

Ernesto had a flashback to that birthday party when Felix Martinez thought he was going to be alone with Linda and Naomi, and suddenly there were his estranged sons. Ernesto and Naomi had worried for weeks about that moment, but it took less than a second for the father and his sons to be in each other's arms.

Ernesto stole a quick look at Mr. Aguilar. His expression was frozen into a hard mask.

"Dawn, *mi hija,*" Mrs. Aguilar whimpered softly. She wiped away a tear. "Are you all right?"

161

"Yes, Mom," Dawn said, going to her mother for a quick kiss. Then she scrambled to her place beside Jorge.

Rachel stared at Dawn with no expression on her face. She seemed stunned that her sister would dare to come here.

"I'm sorry," Dawn finally got out the words. "I'm sorry about everything."

Jorge put his arm around his sister's thin shoulders and gave her a hug.

Ernesto gave Naomi a quick look, and she seemed to share his sinking feeling. This was not going well. Mr. Aguilar did not even look at his daughter.

All during the meal, Ernesto and Abel talked about Cesar Chavez High School and the events coming up. They tried to include Jorge in the conversation, though he was clearly absorbed in his sister's plight.

"Boy, Jorge," Ernesto said in a forced cheery voice, "Coach Muñoz will be glad to have you back in the next track meet. The guy who replaced you bobbled the baton and cost Chavez the relay. Poor guy, he felt terrible, and then leave it to Rod Garcia to rip into him and aggravate his misery. So, with you running again, the Cougars got a better chance."

"Julio Avila is getting better every day," Naomi said. "That guy is going to the Olympics one day. And it's so heartwarming to see his dad out there every time, cheering for his son." Naomi was trying to move the conversation along, but it led to trouble.

"Mr. Avila loves his son very much," Mr. Aguilar said. "A father has a special love for his son as I have for my Jorge. When the son is in danger, a father turns into a ferocious bear." With that, the man cast a hateful look in Dawn's direction.

"Well," Abel said quickly, "it looks like rain next week. I guess we need it, but it's a nuisance."

"My dad hates the rain because it makes the weeds grow," Naomi said in a limp voice.

Ernesto noticed Mrs. Aguilar frequently glancing at Dawn, offering her a little smile.

Dawn's moist eyes filled with gratitude. Jorge looked peaceful and happy. Once, as both Rachel and Dawn reached into the salsa bowl with their chips and bumped hands, Ernesto thought he saw a grudging grin on Rachel's face.

But Mr. Aguilar turned his chair slightly away from the table so he would not have to look at his eldest daughter at all.

CHAPTER TEN

As they drove from the Aguilar house in Ernesto's Nissan, Ernesto said, "It almost worked, didn't it? For a while there I thought maybe …"

Abel shrugged. "Who knows about the future. In the meantime, when Mr. Aguilar is at work, Dawn can come by and have coffee with her mom. She and Jorge can go to Hortencia's. Sometimes that's the way it is, and you gotta live with it."

Naomi nodded. "That's right. Make the best of what is. Don't grieve for what cannot be. That's what my mom always says," Naomi said, looking sad.

They dropped Abel off, and then Ernesto said, "You know, Naomi, I kept thinking of that birthday party when your dad first saw Orlando after all that time. Here your dad is, confronting this boy he was so bitter against. As soon as Orlando was in his face, your dad melted like an ice cream cone in July. It was so beautiful. I don't think I'll ever forget that night." Ernesto shook his head sadly. "I guess I was hoping for something like that."

"Daddy is tough, and he can be mean," Naomi said, "but it's all a crust, Ernie. Beneath that thin crust is a very soft heart. Like over the years, he hasn't always been nice to Mom, but when they told her to come back after that mammogram, you know, to check something out that didn't look right, Daddy just crumpled. I couldn't believe how worried he was.

"And when things turned out okay, he was so grateful that he went out and bought her that amazing diamond necklace and earrings. Dad can be rude and inconsiderate, but he loves deeply. I think that's why during all our family turmoil, I always

166

loved him so much. Even when I was furious at him, I loved him. Always will. Mr. Aguilar is a colder, harder man. He's been tough on Jorge, but I think he loves Jorge more than he loves his daughters. And to think that Dawn would almost ruin his only son's life to protect her boyfriend. He just can't get past that."

"Well, Naomi," Ernesto said, "we're getting closer and closer to graduation, and I think we're all going to make it across the finish line. That senior mentoring program is really paying off. Seniors who were very iffy about graduation are now gonna make it. We've had sixty seniors in that program helping other kids. They helped a hundred and ten seniors.

"The other day I was in Ms. Sanchez's office looking at the computer, and we are way ahead of last year's graduation rate. Last year, we lost seventeen seniors for bad grades. They fell so far behind, they didn't graduate. It makes me so happy we didn't lose any this year."

"That's because we got the best senior class president we've ever had," Naomi said, reaching over and gently pinching Ernesto's shoulder.

"Yeah, I'm proud of starting the mentoring program, but without all those seniors volunteering, it wouldn't have worked. Think of it, sixty kids busy with jobs, classes, sports, social lives, all taking the time to give a hand up to somebody else. These kids have helped somebody graduate, somebody they didn't even know, maybe hadn't spoken to in four years at Chavez," Ernesto said.

"You know, Ernie," Naomi said, "Dawn never graduated from Chavez. She took part in the ceremony, wore her cap and gown, but she'd flunked two classes she needed, and she was supposed to go back to summer school, but she never did. It makes you think. If somebody had helped her, maybe she would have gotten the diploma and never met Adam French."

"Oh man," Ernesto said, "it's the little things."

"Yeah, that's why I'm so proud of what you did here," Naomi said. "You changed lives for the better."

"Awww," Ernesto said. "And maybe you've even forgiven me for dumping Viola now, huh?"

"Oh, I didn't say that," Naomi said. "But I'm starting to bond a little with Nina."

"Nina?" Ernesto asked, taking a moment to get it. "Oh. Nina the Nissan."

"Yeah," Naomi said. "And it isn't like I never see Viola. I often see Yvette tooling around in Viola, taking her mom shopping, taking the girls to school. I always give her a toot on my horn."

Ernesto pulled into the Martinez driveway. He did what he always did, went inside to say "Hi" to the Martinez family. Felix Martinez wasn't home yet from work, and Linda Martinez was out shopping, but the house wasn't empty.

"Zack!" Naomi cried, rushing to her brother and hugging him. "What are you doing here?"

Zack was Naomi's youngest brother. He barely graduated from Chavez High, got in with bad companions, starting to drink and hang out all night. Finally, he tried living on the streets, but his two older brothers, Orlando and Manny, rescued him and took him up to Los Angeles with them. He became a gofer for the Latin band that the other two boys sang and played for. From his text messages home, everything seemed to be going well with Zack.

Now Zack sat slumped in a kitchen chair, drinking a ginger ale. "I hate the music business," he said. His father had wanted him to go to college, but he wouldn't. Then Felix Martinez had enrolled him in an apprentice job where he went to work with his father, wearing a hard hat, working on the construction site. But Zack had gone back to his drinking buddies, and he had begun hanging out at all hours of the night again.

Ernesto had grim memories of trying to get Zack home from a drunken party and almost getting into a fistfight with the other drunks. Ernesto remembered scouring the canyons, looking in the Turkey Neck ravine for Zack, finding him hungry and disheveled. It seemed going up to Los Angeles with his successful brothers was an answer to prayers. At last Zack had a niche.

But now he sat there, his head hanging, his dark eyes heavy with sorrow. "Orlando is doing so good. He's all over YouTube. Manny is going crazy on the drums. He loves it. Their concerts really rock. I envy my brothers. They've found their place, and they're happy. They love the scene. I hate it. I don't want to be racing around from gig to gig, piling on a bus, tearing through the night. They love it. I tried to get with it, but I couldn't. Orlando and Manny, they're good guys. I love them. Nobody ever had better brothers … but …" Zack shook his curly head.

Naomi sat beside her brother, putting her arm around his burly shoulders. Of all the three boys, Zack looked the most like Felix Martinez. Orlando had his father's wild temper, and Zack had his rugged appearance. Manny was in the middle.

"Zack," Naomi said, "you sent such cheery texts."

"Yeah, I didn't want to depress you guys. I've always been a loser, and I didn't want to let you know I still am," Zack said.

"Were Orlando and Manny mad when you left?" Naomi asked.

"Not Manny. He was okay with it. But Orlando was furious. He was yelling how Dad woulda whipped me within an inch of my life if he hadn't intervened the last time I screwed up. Orlando is just like Dad. I think he woulda decked me pretty soon." Zack's voice was low and sorrowful. "I tried to explain to Orlando what I wanted to do with my life, but he screamed at me that I was crazy."

Brutus, the family pit bull came over, and Zack scratched him behind his ears. Brutus loved that. He wagged his tail and looked at Zack sympathetically.

"Where's Mom?" Zack finally asked.

"She's shopping with Ernie's mom. This is their day to go to the mall and have lunch together and pretend they're teenagers again, hanging out. She should be home any minute."

"Dad's still at work, huh? This late? That means he had a bad day. He'll be tired and mean. Been working the forklift all day, and he's looking forward to coming home to a nice peaceful house, and here I am. I think Mom and Dad have been happier since we're all gone. Lot of stress when we were around. Now it's just you and Brutus, Naomi. It's all good.

"And now here I am. The bad penny has returned. What do I tell him? 'Pop, I failed again. I've failed at everything. I'm almost nineteen, and all I've done is screw up.' Only thing I've ever enjoyed is going to the construction site with the old man. I mean, I dug that. The other guys, they seemed like my kind of dudes. I liked having lunch with them, talking sports and stuff. And, you know, this little old house

173

on Bluebird Street. That's what I want when I meet a chick I want to settle down with. A little house like this on a street like this. I want a pickup truck. I want the life my old man has, but he was all over me, bossing me around … like I was still in middle school."

"Zack," Ernesto asked, "you still drinking?"

"Maybe a bottle or a can of beer once in a while, but I haven't been drunk since I left here," Zack said.

Ernesto had a clear memory of the last night Zack spent at the house on Bluebird Street. Ernesto and his father were out for an evening walk when they heard loud fighting. Felix Martinez was trying to stop his drunken son from going out for more partying with his friends. They were in the middle of Bluebird Street going at each other. Luis Sandoval grabbed Mr. Martinez and Ernesto grabbed Zack, separating them. It was then that Orlando came down to get Zack and take him to Los Angeles.

It was a terrible night. Felix Martinez was enraged. Zack was humiliated. All the neighbors were out watching.

Ernesto, Naomi, and Zack all stiffened now at the sound of Felix Martinez's pickup truck coming into the driveway. He was yelling as he got out of the cab.

Zack dropped his face into his hands.

Naomi gently patted her brother on his back.

"Idiots," Felix Martinez was screaming. "They give me idiots to work with! Where do they get these people? Thirty stories up, and they don't know what they're doing. I'd do better work with a tribe of monkeys."

Mr. Martinez pushed his way through the front door, and then he stopped cold. He saw his son.

"Zack, what are you doing here?" he cried.

"I got tired of the music business, Pop," Zack said. "I don't fit in there. Orlando was real mad at me for leaving but I couldn't take it anymore."

"How'd you get here?" Mr. Martinez asked. "I don't see no car."

"I took the bus from LA, and then I took the city bus to Washington and walked the rest of the way," Zack said. "I shoulda let you guys know I was coming. But it just hit me all of a sudden. I didn't belong there. I belong here. I see all the skyscrapers going up around town … and you're part of that, Pop, and that's awesome. I thought maybe …" His voice trailed off. His worried eyes searched his father's face. Ernesto and Naomi sat there in silence.

Felix Martinez glanced over at them. "You guys know this was coming down?" he asked.

"No," Ernesto said. "I was bringing Naomi home when we saw Zack. I was … uh … surprised."

"Yeah," Naomi said. "I was shocked. All his texts were so positive."

Felix Martinez took a deep breath. "What are you sayin', boy? Give it to me straight. I had a rough day. They sent me all the stupid people to do the work today, to get the materials way up there. Tell me what's happening here," he said.

"I screwed up here before, Pop. I know that. I'm so ashamed of that last night when I was so drunk. I swung at you. That was awful, Pop. I'm sorry. I mean, I don't blame you if you want no part of me. But I was thinking maybe if there was an apprentice slot open where you work, I wouldn't mind the lowest kind of work, as long as I was part of the team.

"I wasn't happy in school. I was miserable up there with my brothers and their gigs, but those few weeks I worked with you on the construction site, Pop, I was happy. I'd get up excited every morning. I know I screwed up, hanging with my friends, but I'm not like that anymore. I don't have no-good friends. I sometimes have a beer, but not often and then just one. I never get drunk anymore, Pop. Never. I swear it," Zack said.

Felix Martinez sat down. He looked at

177

Ernesto and said, "Is this really happening? Ernie, is this a dream I'm having? I worked too hard today. Maybe I'm hallucinating."

"Do you … uh … still have my hard hat, Pop?" Zack asked. "I was so happy to put that on. I was proud of it. I've matured, Pop. I'm not the kid you remember. I know what I want now. I want a good job doing a man's work. I want to be proud of what I do. I want to do what you do, Pop, build things, important buildings that people need. I want to meet a chick someday and live in a house like this one. I want kids and a regular life. You got a good gig here, Pop, and if you'd let me …" His voice was shaking.

"Yeah, I still got your hard hat," Felix Martinez said. "And if you're crazy enough to follow the old man in construction, I can get you in. You can do like me, freeze in the winter, roast in the summer heat, work with idiots who don't know their right hand from their left. You can work like a dog and get a bad back like me, sure. I can do that for you, Zack."

"I promise you, Pop, I'm not the stupid kid who left here that night. Nothing like what happened that night will ever happen again. I'll learn everything I need, and I'll work really hard. I'll be the best guy on that construction site, Pop. I'm not the kid who left here a few months ago," Zack said.

Felix Martinez smiled. "I'm not the dude who saw you leave that night either, kid. I understand something I didn't get then. You're not my little *muchacho* no more. You're a man. A man don't need bossing around. A man don't need his backside whipped. I got that now."

Zack and his father got up almost at once. They rushed at each other and were in each other's arms, laughing and shoving each other.

Just then, Linda Martinez came in the door. She dropped all her shopping bags on the floor and screamed, "*Mi hijo!*"

Zack grabbed his mother and hugged and kissed her. "I'm home, Mama," he shouted.

Ernesto looked at Naomi and grinned. "Time for me to go, babe. See you!"

On the weekend, Ernesto and Naomi were sitting in the little garden Felix Martinez had built behind the house on Bluebird Street. He had carved chipmunks and rabbits and little elves. Some of them looked like the seven dwarfs, and some just looked like strange little trolls. There was a tiny waterfall that gurgled merrily all the time and a pond. Ernesto loved the place. It always amazed him that a man as rough as Felix Martinez could have made such a lovely, whimsical place. But lately, he had begun to understand. This was the gentle, tender side of the man coming out.

It was an early spring day, and everything was blooming. There seemed to be a brightness to everything, a kind of glow. Naomi sat on the same bench as Ernesto and rested her head on his shoulder.

"Ernie, do you think Mr. Aguilar will ever accept Dawn?" Naomi asked.

"Yeah, but I think it's going to take some time. You can't guilt trip him into it. He has legit reasons for feeling like he does. I mean, Dawn somehow guilt-tripped Jorge into covering for her boyfriend. But I guess I understand why he felt so loyal. I think old Aguilar will come around soon. He does love his daughter."

"Brothers and sisters have a complicated relationship, huh? Look at Penny and Abel. Me and Orlando, Manny, and Zack. Even you! I know you don't want Katalina and Juanita to grow up, but it's going to happen."

Ernie sighed. "I know, but I want them to be little girls for a while longer."

"Ernie," Naomi said, "do you ever imagine what it will be like for us ten years from now?"

"Yeah, Juanita will be finishing high school, and my sister Katalina will be in college. Little Alfredo will be playing baseball and probably riding his skateboard. Mom will have written a bunch of books, and Dad maybe will be teaching full time at college, or maybe he'll be principal at Chavez. I'll be a lawyer here in the *barrio,* and I'll love my work. People will trust me like they trust Uncle Arturo," Ernesto said.

"My brother Orlando will be a famous singer and Manny a terrific drummer. Dad will finally be foreman, and he and Zack will be working together. I'll be working on a medical research team at some university. Remember when Cruz Lopez's mom died so young, leaving a brokenhearted family, those little kids? I made up my mind right then that I'd go into medical research, and I hope to be part of the team that makes a breakthrough on the terrible disease that killed Mrs. Lopez," Naomi said.

Naomi reached for Ernesto's hand and said softly, "Our children will play right here. They'll laugh at Dad's cute elves and stick their fingers in the waterfall. Dad will make such a wonderful grandfather, and Mom will make a wonderful grandma. Your parents too. Your mom can read her children's books to our kids, and your dad can take them for walks like you and he do."

They moved closer to each other until they were in each other's arms then.

"We'll be like this, Ernie, forever and always," Naomi said, kissing Ernesto's cheeks and then his lips.

"I love you, babe, and I always will," Ernesto said.

"Love you more," Naomi whispered.

They clung to each other. Ernesto held Naomi so close that their slender, athletic young bodies seemed to merge until they were just one person.